by

Jay Northcote

*Lots of love
Jay x*

Copyright

Cover artist: Garrett Leigh.
Editor: Sue Adams.
Helping Hand © 2015 Jay Northcote.

ALL RIGHTS RESERVED

This literary work may not be reproduced or transmitted in any form or by any means, including electronic or photographic reproduction, in whole or in part, without express written permission.
This is a work of fiction and any resemblance to persons, living or dead, or business establishments, events or locales is coincidental.
The Licensed Art Material is being used for illustrative purposes only.
All Rights Are Reserved. No part of this may be used or reproduced in any manner whatsoever without written permission, except in the case of brief quotations embodied in critical articles and reviews.

This book contains material that is intended for a mature, adult audience. It contains graphic language, explicit sexual content, and adult situations.

To Justyna.
Thank you for the cheerleading. This story would probably have never seen the light of day if it weren't for your support.

Chapter One

Jez flipped idly through the channels on the TV as he munched on the bland, slightly soggy pizza that had been on special offer in the supermarket. It tasted like shit.

"For fuck's sake, just pick something and stick with it. You're driving me crazy." Mac—aka James MacKenzie, aka Big Mac to his mates—grumbled from the dining table, where he had books and notes for their current assignment spread out in front of him.

They were on the same course—Geography, and Jez had already finished his and handed it in early, but Mac was only halfway through.

"You could work in your room, dickhead, or go to the library if you want peace and quiet," Jez said, but his tone was mild.

"I prefer it down here. Working on a Saturday night is bad enough without being shut away on my own as well."

Jez settled on *The Simpsons* and put the remote aside.

The living room door opened and Shawn put his sandy blond head around it. "Me and Mike are heading out soon. Are you sure you don't wanna come and meet us later? We're going clubbing after the pub. There'll be tons of freshers out tonight; pulling will be like shooting fish in a barrel. All those girls straight from the arms of their parents ready for their first taste of freedom—and by 'freedom,' I mean my dick."

Jez rolled his eyes. "In your dreams, Shawny. And no. I'm skint, remember? So unless you want to buy all my drinks tonight, it's never gonna happen."

"What about you, Big Mac?"

Mac ran his hand over his short dark hair and didn't glance up from his laptop. "Nope. I've got this essay on river systems to get done by Tuesday."

"Aw, come on, man. It's Saturday night. Can't it wait till tomorrow?"

Mac clenched his jaw and flushed as he shook his head, looking down at his notes and shuffling the papers around. "No."

"But—"

"Give him a break, Shawn," Jez said, a steely thread of warning in his voice. "I'm sure you and Mike can manage without us."

Jez, Mac, Shawn, and Mike had lived in the same corridor last year, and had soon gravitated towards each other and started hanging out together. At the start of the year, they'd all gone out a lot, checking out all the popular student pubs and clubs in Plymouth, but Mike and Shawn hadn't gone quite as crazy as Jez and Mac, who kept up the partying right through till the summer. By the end of their first year, Jez had racked up an enormous overdraft and his parents flatly refused to bail him out even though they could easily afford it. Mac got behind with his studies, been late for a couple of assignments, and then nearly flunked the end-of-year exams. So now, at the start of their second year, Jez and Mac had decided to rein in the partying, and Jez wasn't going to stand by and watch Shawn give Mac a hard time about it.

Shawn met Jez's gaze and obviously decided it wasn't worth arguing.

He shrugged instead and said with a grin, "Okay, whatever. Later, losers."

"Have fun," Jez said.

"Oh, we will." Shawn banged the door shut behind him.

"Thanks," Mac said, his brown eyes serious and levelled on Jez.

"You're welcome."

Jez finished his pizza and then settled himself more comfortably on the sofa, lying sideways with his head propped up on a cushion. He could hear the tap of Mac's fingers on his laptop keys and the occasional scratch of a pen and rustle of paper as he worked, but it didn't bother him. As Mac said, it was a bit sad being stuck in on Saturday night, and so he was glad of Mac's company. They had an easy relationship—a solid, casual friendship based on spending lots of time in each other's company over the past year.

The house they lived in was a large rental with six bedrooms. On a weeknight there were usually a few of them around, hanging out in the living room or getting in each other's way in the kitchen. But tonight Jez and Mac were the only ones who'd stayed in. Dani, the only girl who lived with them, was away this weekend visiting her boyfriend, and Josh, the fifth guy in the house, was usually out every Friday and Saturday. He tended to do his own thing rather than socialise with the rest of them at weekends. Josh was gay, so his hangouts were rather different from the rest of them.

An hour or so later, Mac finally closed his laptop. "That's it. I'm done for tonight. I need a drink."

Jez watched as Mac stood and stretched, his back cracking as he raised his arms over his head and arched back. His T-shirt rose to show enviable abs and a line of dark hair leading down to his jeans.

"It's only nine," Jez said. "You gonna go out after all?" A twinge of disappointment licked at the edges of his consciousness. It really would suck to be the only one stuck in on a Saturday night.

"Nah. I can't be arsed. And Lucy will probably be out, and she's still pissed off with me for breaking up with her. I could do without the aggro. I've got a few beers in the fridge. D'you want one?"

"I won't be able to pay you back, not for a while anyway." Jez had managed to get a part-time job — a few shifts in a local café — but every penny of that was going to pay off his debts.

"That's okay. It's only cheap stuff, and I did all that work for my dad over the summer."

Mac's dad was a builder, and he paid Mac a decent wage when Mac helped him out.

"Okay, then. Cheers."

Mac came back a minute or so later with a four-pack of lager. "Shift your arse," he said.

"There is a whole other sofa you know."

"Yeah, but this one has the best view of the telly."

Jez moved his legs reluctantly, turning and putting them up on the coffee table to make space for Mac in the other corner of the large three-seater.

"This beats paying for overpriced beer in a crowded pub anyway," Mac said. "I meant it when I said I was going to stop going out every weekend this year."

"Yeah?" Jez hadn't been sure Mac was committed to the plan. For Jez, it was a necessity. He simply couldn't afford to carry on like he had last year.

"I'm on my last chance," Mac's voice was serious. "My tutor called me in for a meeting on the first day back. If I fuck up this year, then I'm out."

"Shit, really?" Jez hadn't realised it was that bad.

"Yeah. And I'm not one of those people who can dash off an essay in an evening and still get a good grade. I need to put the time in." Jez flushed, feeling guilty because he *was* one of those people. "So," Mac continued. "I decided this term I'm not going out much at all. I'm focusing on work, and relaxation isn't going to involve late nights and hangovers that make me miss lectures. A few beers in front of the TV is gonna be my limit. It'll be hard to stick to it, but I want to try."

"Let's make a pact," Jez said. "We'll both do it. Between now and Christmas, we won't go out drinking every weekend for the sake of it, only on special occasions—like birthdays and stuff. It'll be easier if we both do it."

"Safety in numbers?" Mac grinned.

"Something like that. We can help each other stay strong when Shawn and Mike pester us."

"Okay, it's a deal." Mac raised his can, and Jez bumped it with his own.

"Deal."

They sat in companionable silence for a while, finishing their drinks while they watched TV before starting on a second.

"So, how come you broke up with Lucy?" Jez asked. "I thought you seemed pretty into her back in the summer."

Mac shrugged. "I dunno. I just wasn't feeling it, you know? She wanted to get serious, and I wasn't ready."

"You wanted to stay young, free, and single?"

"Something like that." Mac snorted in amusement and Jez turned to see his grin. "But I'm not exactly making the most of it, am I? Staying in with you instead of going out on the pull."

"Yeah." Jez grinned back. "Are you regretting our pact already? It's not too late. You could still go and catch up with the others."

"Hey, you're not supposed to be encouraging me." Mac sounded affronted. "But I'm tired anyway, and pulling's too much like hard work. It's easier to stay in and have a wank. My right hand's a sure thing. There's no risk of crashing and burning there."

Jez chuckled. "Truth."

"I miss blow jobs, though. Lucy was bloody good at that." Mac's voice was wistful, and he gazed into space, clearly lost in fantasy. His cheeks flushed a little as he continued, and Jez felt a rush of answering heat in his groin.

"Yeah?" Jez's voice came out a little hoarse. Fuck, he was getting hard. Damn Mac and his talk of wanking and blow jobs. His head was full of images of Mac getting his dick sucked, and Jez wasn't quite sure why the idea of that was doing it for him. It never had before. Even though Jez had had a few sexual experiences with other boys at boarding school, he'd always considered himself straight, because he definitely liked girls.

There was a long pause. The TV chattered away, but neither of them paid any attention to it. Mac was a million miles away, and Jez was staring at him, his heart beating fast. He dropped his gaze to Mac's lap. The bulge in his tracksuit bottoms gave him away. Jez was relieved he wasn't the only one popping an inappropriate boner.

Suddenly Mac snapped back into reality. He cleared his throat and stood up, adjusting the tent in his trousers. Jez stared—he couldn't help himself— and when he dragged his gaze back to Mac's face, Mac was watching him. The air between them felt charged. Jez wondered if it was all him, or whether Mac felt it too.

Mac finally broke the silence. "I'm, uh…. I'm gonna head up to bed." He was still blushing.

"Time for that hot date with your right hand?" Jez smirked, trying to ease the tension back to something recognisable and familiar.

"Yeah. Something like that."

Jez hit the off button on the TV remote. "All this talk has made me horny too. I might join you in a minute." Mac's eyes flew wide open at that, and the shock on his face made Jez burst out laughing. "Not literally, you twat."

Mac's face had turned an even darker shade of scarlet. "Fuck off." He flipped Jez off. "Good night, loser." He turned away.

"Night, Mac. Have fun with Mr Right."

Jez watched Mac as he left the room, all big shoulders and slim hips. No wonder the girls always chased him.

He left it a few minutes before following Mac up the stairs. Jez paused on the landing; Mac's room was next to his on the top floor. He listened, but the muffled sound of music covered any other noises. He wondered if Mac was watching porn or whacking off to the fantasies in his own head, and if so, what those fantasies might be. Then he wondered why he was thinking about his housemate jerking off. Shaking his head at himself, Jez went into his own room to take care of business and tried to keep Mac out of his head while he did it.

He mostly succeeded.

Chapter Two

The following Friday night, they were the only ones left in again.

They'd both stayed in all week, but this was the first time they'd had the house to themselves. During the week there was usually someone else around.

Jez had been out for a run in the early evening and came back to find Mac in the living room working on another assignment — one that Jez had finished in the library at lunchtime.

"Do you need any help with it?" Jez offered.

"No thanks. I'm nearly finished, but if you don't mind reading it through for me once I'm done, that would be cool. Check I haven't said anything stupid."

Once Jez had showered and eaten, Mac was packing his books away.

"Do you still want me to read it?"

"Yeah, cheers."

Jez sat on the sofa with Mac's laptop. He made a few comments in the margin as he went.

"Looks good," he said when he got to the end. "But—"

Mac groaned. "I knew there'd be a but."

Jez grinned. "Nothing major. I fixed a few typos and left you some notes. I just reckon it would flow better if you changed the order of your paragraphs. It makes more sense that way. And you could develop your conclusion a little more, perhaps."

"Okay, thanks."

Mac spent another half hour reworking it. When he was finally done, he joined Jez on the sofa to watch TV. He offered Jez a beer again, and Jez accepted.

"Cheers. I'll get some next weekend," Jez promised. Now he'd cut right down on his spending, he could stretch to a few cheap drinks at the weekend.

There was a film just starting — some American cop drama that Jez had never heard of.

They watched the film as they worked their way through a couple of beers. Despite the action on the screen, Jez was distracted. His mind kept wandering back to the conversation they'd had last weekend. Since then, Mac had been in Jez's thoughts more than he was comfortable with.

Given his sexual history, Jez had always known he was capable of getting off with guys. But when he was at school, he had figured it was about availability. Having another willing person to lend a helping hand — or occasionally a mouth if you were lucky — made sense in the all-male environment where he had spent his adolescence. Lock hundreds of teenage boys together in a boarding school and gay stuff was going to happen sometimes. But doing it didn't mean you *were* gay. Jez was definitely interested in girls too, so once he was old enough to have a little more freedom and opportunity, he'd focused on them instead and relegated his same-sex adventures to past experience. He had always reckoned he wouldn't mind experimenting with a guy again if the occasion arose, but he hadn't given it a lot of thought.

Now it was all he could think about. Something about last Saturday night had flipped a switch in Jez's brain, and he was looking at Mac in a whole new way.

Mac drained his second beer, unaware that Jez was watching him. Jez's eyes tracked the bob of Mac's throat as he swallowed, then dropped down to study Mac's strong, long-fingered hand where it curled loosely around the empty can.

"Want another one?" Mac asked.

Jez tore his gaze away from Mac's hand and up to meet his eyes. "If you're sure you don't mind?" Jez had drunk fast tonight, and he was enjoying the buzz of the alcohol. Apart from last Saturday, he had hardly drunk for a couple of weeks and relished the familiar tendrils of warm relaxation that crept through his system.

When Mac returned with more beer, the female undercover cop in the film was getting it on with some bloke she was trying to get information from.

"Whoa, she's hot," Mac said appreciatively as he took his place next to Jez again.

"She really is." Jez watched, transfixed, as the woman on the screen kissed her way down the guy's chest, her hair falling over her face in a curtain that hid the guy's crotch as she moved lower still, keeping it respectable enough for the censors. But Jez's brain filled in the gaps, and by the time the camera cut to the guy's face, Jez's dick was growing hard, and his cheeks flushed hot as arousal swept through him in a heady rush.

"Nice," Mac said. His voice had a rough edge to it.

A movement in Jez's peripheral vision made him glance sideways in time to see Mac adjusting himself.

"Yeah." Jez looked away quickly, just in time to catch the expression of ecstasy on the actor's face before it faded to black.

Fuck.

Jez was so turned on. He almost wished Mac had gone out, because then Jez could have got his dick out right then and had the wank he was desperate for. He surreptitiously pressed his hand against his erection through his trousers, biting the inside of his cheek and trying not to give himself away by breathing too hard. His mind flashed back to a few occasions at school where he and some other boys had jerked off together — to sex scenes in films or to porn.

Afterwards, Jez blamed the alcohol for loosening his tongue, because he didn't think about it before he spoke. The words tumbled out before he could stop them.

"Man, I'm seriously horny now. Have you got any decent porn on that laptop?"

"Huh?" Mac snapped his head around to meet Jez's gaze. Jez's heart pounded erratically, but his dick was still standing to attention. "What… you mean, you want to wank in here? *Now*? Wouldn't that be weird?" Mac sounded seriously freaked out.

Jez backtracked quickly, cheeks hot. "It doesn't have to be weird. I've done it before with guys at school, and it's never been a big deal. But don't worry about it. I'll go and watch my own stash instead. But I need something soon, 'cause I'm gonna explode after watching that sex scene."

Jez was expecting an instant no from Mac. He wouldn't have blamed him. A lot of guys wouldn't be into what Jez was suggesting. Jez's heart still thumped hard, but his arousal didn't abate despite his anxiety. He was shocked by how much he wanted this.

Mac bit his lip and frowned. "Seriously. You've done that?"

Jez shrugged, trying to look nonchalant. "Yeah. Like I said, it was no big deal. Just guys messing around."

Mac stared a moment longer, then he stood, and Jez's heart sank as he walked away. But Mac only went to fetch his laptop from the dining table. He sat back down and then opened it and tapped in his password.

"What sort of stuff do you wanna watch?" Mac's voice was gruff and he focused on the screen rather than Jez.

Fuck. They were really going to do this, then.

"Uh, I don't know. Whatever floats your boat. I'm not that fussy." It was true. Jez's tastes in porn were pretty eclectic. He couldn't imagine Mac watching anything that wouldn't do it for him.

"Okay." Mac opened his bookmarks and clicked on something. "This girl's pretty hot." He put the laptop down on the coffee table.

Jez picked up the TV remote, paused the film, and then moved closer to Mac so he could see the laptop screen better. Their thighs touched, and the warmth of Mac's leg, even through layers of clothing, set Jez's nerve endings alight.

There was an awkward silence as they started watching the action on the screen. It was a straight-down-to-business kind of scene: no distracting storyline, backing music, or bad acting. There was simply a sexy girl in office clothes and a guy in a suit kissing and undressing each other. The only sounds were the rustle of their clothes and the wet noises of kissing. Jez was aware of the sound of his own breath and of Mac next to him. Neither of them made a move to do anything, but Jez was painfully turned on, and sitting here in uncomfortable silence, watching porn and *not* jerking off, was getting seriously awkward. Someone had to get this party started, and as it had been Jez's suggestion in the first place, he figured Mac was probably waiting for him to make the first move, so to speak.

The girl dropped to her knees, and the guy's dick was front and centre on the screen. Porn-star huge, of course, and rock-hard. Jez finally gave in to the need for friction and started to rub his erection through the soft, stretchy fabric of his jogging bottoms as the girl licked up the underside, and the guy on the screen groaned appreciatively. He imagined how it would feel to have someone doing that to him. It had been way too long: weeks… months, even.

Mac shifted next to him, his elbow bumping Jez's ribs as his hand started to move over the bulge in his jeans. Jez snuck a quick glance sideways. That couldn't be comfortable. Mac's dick must be trapped behind the zip if he was properly hard now.

"Fuck it." Jez pulled his cock out of his trousers and started stroking in earnest, nearly groaning with relief as his hand finally gripped and slid exactly as he wanted it. He let his head fall back and bit his lip, and his eyes fluttered closed for a moment before he opened them again to watch the action as the guy on the screen got his dick worshipped.

Mac froze beside him, his arm stilling for a moment, but Jez ignored him. There was no way he was going to stop now. His hand felt too good, and Mac had had plenty of chances to duck out. If he wasn't going to join in, that was his problem. He could watch Jez getting off. Jez was past caring.

The sound of Mac's zip and the rustle of clothing cut through the fog of Jez's arousal. Jez couldn't help his gaze sliding sideways again. It was natural curiosity to want to see what Mac looked like hard. He'd seen him naked once or twice—in changing rooms or the showers at the gym where they worked out together sometimes—and he knew Mac had a nice-looking dick even when it was soft.

"Wow." Jez stared in disbelief. Big Mac certainly earned his nickname.

"What?"

"You're hung like a donkey." Jez stared, an uncomfortable mix of envy and arousal flaring in the pit of his belly.

"You're supposed to be watching the porn, not me," Mac said, but he sounded amused rather than uncomfortable and his hand moved on his cock, sliding slowly up and down, pulling the foreskin back to expose the dark pink head.

"I'm just checking out the competition." Jez reluctantly tore his gaze away and looked back at the screen, where the guy's rather less fascinating cock was still getting worked over by the girl.

After that, they stopped talking. The silence was only punctuated by the occasional moan or "Yeah baby" from the laptop, the rasp of their own breathing, and the sound of skin-on-skin.

Jez was achingly aware of every part of him that was in contact with Mac: the press of his thigh, the bump of Mac's elbow against his arm. Jez couldn't resist sneaking the occasional look sideways. Mac's dick was fascinating in its thick perfection. The sound of Mac's hand on it was getting louder—sticky, wet sounds as he obviously got closer to coming. Jez was close, too, but he didn't want to be distracted by his own orgasm. He wanted to see Mac come first.

Jez had no clue what was happening on the laptop screen any longer. He was far too focused on Mac, on the sounds he was making and the feel of his movements so close to Jez's body. Even when he looked at the screen, it could have been *Match of the Day* for all he cared. Finally Mac gasped and stiffened, and Jez turned to watch as Mac came. Mac hunched forward, biting back a moan and catching his spunk in the palm of his free hand.

That was all it took for Jez. The sight of Mac coming and the little sounds he made tipped Jez over into blissful release.

"Fuck, yes," he hissed, gaze still fixed on Mac's dick as he shot all over his T-shirt, too lost in the pleasure to care about making a mess. He collapsed back, closing his eyes and panting as the waves of his climax receded.

The sofa shifted as Mac moved beside him, and then the sound of the porn on the laptop stopped as the lid clicked shut.

"Bollocks," Mac muttered.

Jez opened his eyes to see Mac staring at the sticky mess in his left hand.

Jez chuckled. "We didn't plan this very well." He tucked his cock away, then sat up and stripped off his T-shirt. "Here." He passed it to Mac. "It'll be going in the wash anyway. I jizzed all over it."

Mac wiped his hand on a dry bit of the T-shirt, then balled it up and passed it back. "Cheers." Mac's cheeks were pink, and he licked his lips. He avoided Jez's eyes, but his gaze slid over Jez's torso in a way that left a tingle in its wake. He zipped his jeans back up. "I'm gonna go to bed now."

"Okay." Jez deliberately kept his tone light. Mac looked like a spooked animal, and Jez didn't want to say anything to make him more uncomfortable. Maybe if he acted like this was a completely normal thing for two straight guys to do on a quiet night in, Mac wouldn't freak out and make things uncomfortable. "Night, man. Sleep well."

"You too," Mac mumbled as he departed, laptop under one arm and his back to Jez.

Chapter Three

Jez's hopes of carrying on as normal were dashed to pieces the next day. He didn't see Mac until late morning, and when they eventually crossed paths in the kitchen, Jez greeted him just like he normally would with an "All right, mate," and a grin, but Mac wouldn't look him in the eye.

Mac muttered a quick hi and turned away from Jez to rifle through the fridge. Jez stared at his back for a moment and then decided this wasn't his problem. It wasn't as if he'd coerced Mac into anything. Mac was a big boy, capable of making his own decisions. It stung a little that Mac so clearly regretted this one, but whatever. He'd get over it eventually, and Jez wasn't going to lose any sleep in the meantime.

Jez took his tea through to the living room and sat on the empty sofa. Dani was in the corner of the other sofa, eating noodles, with her long purple hair tucked behind her ears. Josh, with dark shadows under his eyes, was curled up at the other end reading and making notes. He'd been out all night. Jez had been eating breakfast when Josh let himself in and headed straight for the coffee. When Jez asked if he'd had a good night, Josh had grunted noncommittally, so Jez hadn't pressed him.

Mac joined them without a word, carrying a huge plate of sandwiches and a glass of milk. He crossed the room to sit in the armchair rather than taking the space beside Jez.

"Is it okay if I put the TV on?" he asked Josh, who was lost in his book with a frown of concentration on his sharp features.

"Yeah, fine." The silver ring in Josh's lip glinted as he glanced up and gave Mac a quick smile.

Mike drifted downstairs around lunchtime, hung-over and tired, followed shortly by Shawn, who was in an even worse state.

"You look rough, Shawny," Jez said. "Good night, was it?"

"Awesome." Shawn grinned, then lifted his jaw to proudly show an angry red mark on his neck. "Look."

"Jesus, did you pull a vampire?" Dani teased.

"She was *very* into me. What can I say?"

All six of them hung out in the living room most of the afternoon. It was raining outside, and none of them had any plans, so they enjoyed a lazy Sunday of TV, banter, and a bit of studying for those who had deadlines. The whole afternoon Jez didn't manage to catch Mac's eye once, and it wasn't for want of trying. He made a point of including him in the conversation, mentioning the film they'd watched last night to try and get him to interact. But even when he joined in the conversation, Mac looked at anyone rather than Jez. The awkwardness between them was painfully obvious to Jez, but nobody else seemed to notice. If they did, they didn't comment.

Eventually, by late afternoon, Jez was fed up with it. Making the excuse of needing to call his family, he went up to his room and hid out there for the evening, only going back down to grab some dinner, which he ate upstairs. He didn't see Mac again that night.

As the week progressed, Jez saw little of Mac.

Considering they were on the same course and normally sat together, it was impressive that Mac managed to avoid him all week. He left the house early instead of walking in to lectures with Jez and spent a lot of time studying in the library rather than at home.

When their paths crossed in the communal spaces in the house, Jez made the effort to act normally around him. As far as Jez was concerned, nothing needed to change. What they'd done together was a bit of fun and nothing to stress about — but that didn't mean Jez could forget about it. He didn't *want* to forget about it. It had been seriously hot, and even if it was a one-off, he'd be filing it away in his own personal spank bank for years to come.

Jez was frustrated at the distance between them, but he didn't think pushing would fix it. He went out running on Wednesday afternoon to burn off some excess energy and his irritation at Mac's avoidance. The weather had turned much cooler. It was early October, and they were well into autumn now. He ran through town and up over the Hoe, where a stiff sea breeze whipped his hair and a few drops of rain stung his cheeks. The sea was choppy and murky grey, reflecting Jez's mood. Shaking it off, he picked up his pace, heading out along the sea front before finally circling back home.

That night he slept better than he had in days.

As the weekend approached, Mac started to relax around Jez again, and they fell back into the easy friendship they'd enjoyed before. On Friday, Mac took his usual seat beside Jez again in their morning lecture, and Jez welcomed him with a nod and a smile. The professor droned on about glaciers, and Jez was distracted — and he wasn't the only one. He caught Mac staring at him a couple of times, and then Mac would flush and look away quickly, obviously still embarrassed about what had happened.

They stayed in together on Friday night when all the others had plans — alone again for the first time all week. Jez was half expecting Mac to hide out in his room and avoid him, and he was relieved when that didn't happen. Instead Mac joined him in the living room in front of the TV, and they ended up watching *The Walking Dead* on DVD.

"Do you want a drink?" Jez held up the half-full pint glass. "I got some cider because it was on special offer. It tastes a bit rough, but it does the job." Jez was in the mood for the buzz of alcohol tonight. It might ease the awkwardness between them.

"Yeah, thanks."

Jez went to the kitchen to get the cider and another glass for Mac. He'd bought a couple of two-litre bottles, deciding that even with his economy drive he could treat himself to a few drinks at the weekend. Plus he owed Mac from the weekend before.

They watched a few episodes back to back. Jez refilled their glasses whenever they were empty and got the second bottle from the kitchen when they finished the first one. As the alcohol seeped through Jez's system, he felt warm and relaxed. He found himself slumping sideways, half leaning on Mac's solid bulk beside him. It was comfortable, and Mac made no move to put any distance between them. Jez was relieved that things were okay again. He'd missed Mac this week while Mac was being weird.

Mac's glass was sitting empty on the coffee table again, so Jez leaned forward and unscrewed the cap on the second bottle. It fizzed up as he poured it, making a frothy white head that filled the top third of the glass.

"Oops." He handed the glass to Mac, and their fingers brushed, the warm contact making Jez's belly fizz like the cider.

"Thanks." Mac's smile was lazy and open. He hadn't smiled at Jez like that since last weekend.

Jez grinned back, losing himself in the beautiful stretch of Mac's lips and the crinkles at the corners of his dark brown eyes. "You're welcome."

"Are you trying to get me drunk?" Mac asked. His smile turned teasing, flirtatious almost.

Jez felt his cheeks heat as he held Mac's gaze for a few exciting, uncomfortable seconds. "Maybe."

He sat back again, watching the screen but no longer taking any of it in. His attention was all on the warmth of Mac's thigh alongside his and the solid press of his shoulder. Jez breathed in and caught Mac's scent: clean laundry and shower gel, but beneath that the woodsy scent of skin—warm male skin. It reminded Jez of school locker rooms, wrestling with his mates, and unwanted adolescent erections. He remembered the sounds of Mac's hand on his cock last weekend and the stifled moan when he came, and—

Fuck.

Jez's cock tingled as it swelled and thickened. Beside him Mac laughed at something on the TV and took another long swallow from his glass.

Jez followed suit, draining what was left in his with a few large gulps, and then he stood. Brave—or stupid—from alcohol and horniness, he turned to Mac, not bothering to try and hide the obvious line of his semi in his tracksuit bottoms. "I'm gonna go and watch some porn and have a wank. Do you want to come?" As soon as the words were out of his mouth, he realised what he'd said and snorted, adding, "No pun intended."

Jez's accidental double meaning made the moment less awkward than it might have been, and Mac laughed, but then he flushed and his gaze slid down Jez's torso to his bulge and back before he spoke.

"In your room?" His expression was wary.

"Yeah, that's where my laptop is, and I'm not sure I want to make a habit of spanking the monkey in the living room."

But I wouldn't mind making a habit of doing it with you.

He managed to resist the urge to say those words out loud. He hadn't had enough cider to completely obliterate his verbal filter, thankfully. Mac was still staring at him but not moving.

"Okay, I'm going." Jez turned away, regretting having made the suggestion. They'd only just got back to normal after last weekend, and now Mac would probably spend the next week avoiding him again. He felt stupid for suggesting it after Mac's obvious discomfort all week.

But the TV switched off as he reached the door, and he heard Mac's footsteps behind him. Jez grinned but didn't turn around, and as Mac followed him up the stairs, Jez was buzzing with excitement, his arousal building at the thought of what was about to happen.

In Jez's room Mac hung back while Jez picked up his laptop and made himself comfortable on the double bed. Mac waited uncertainly until Jez patted the space next to him.

"I can't believe I'm doing this again," Mac said, but he joined Jez on the bed as Jez typed in his password and pulled up his porn bookmarks.

"It's no big deal." Jez shrugged, trying to reassure him. Although Jez wasn't sure he managed to convince Mac or even himself. This wasn't the same as a group of lads jerking off to porn. The fact that there were only two of them added a layer of intimacy that couldn't be denied. But Jez didn't want to examine it too closely right now. He just wanted to get off.

"This one's good." Jez clicked on a fairly standard porn vid that he often jerked off to. It was straight-up porn, nothing kinky, and the girl was pretty and looked like she was enjoying it. He was aware of Mac beside him, his body tense and his breathing shallow. Jez wondered why Mac had agreed to this when he was obviously a million miles out of his comfort zone. Outwardly ignoring him, Jez took the lead again and was the first to start touching himself. He leaned back against the headboard and palmed his stiffening dick through his trousers, forcing himself to relax as the building rush of anticipation flooded through him. He'd forgotten how hot it was jerking off with company. Maybe he was an exhibitionist and liked putting on a show? Perhaps next time he hooked up with a girl he could try doing it for her if she was into it and see if it felt as good as it did doing this with Mac.

A rustle of clothing beside him brought his attention back to Mac. Jez saw movement out of the corner of his eye, and a quick glance confirmed that Mac had his hand shoved down the front of his pyjama bottoms.

Jez bit back the urge to encourage him; he didn't want to spook him. Instead he pulled out his own cock and started to stroke it in earnest, not even trying to hide the hitch in his breathing as he gave in to the pleasure that surged through him. He kept the movement slow. If he let himself, he could probably come in a matter of minutes, but he wanted to make this last. Who knew if he'd ever talk Mac into this again? Jez didn't want it to be over too soon.

Mac took a deep breath and let it out, slow and shaky. Then the bed shifted as he raised his arse up enough to push his pyjamas down a little. Jez couldn't help himself; he had to look. For some reason Mac was much more fascinating than the people on the laptop screen. Jez glanced sideways, trying not to be obvious about it, and squeezed his own dick as he saw how hard Mac was already. He was stiff and shiny-wet at the tip, and Jez wanted to feel it in his hand—or even in his mouth. He'd done that a few times for his roommate when he was sixteen, but at the time he'd been ashamed to admit it turned him on, because he was only swapping favours with a friend. He wasn't *gay*. He'd buried that memory deep, but the sight of Mac's thick cock made his mouth water and his balls ache.

Jez tore his eyes away and stared at the screen again, but his attention was still on Mac even though his gaze wasn't.

Jez was close now; his runaway thoughts had pushed him closer. He bit his lip and tried to fight it, but unless he stopped, he was going to get to the point of no return very soon.

"Fuck," he muttered, lifting his T-shirt up out of the way. He threw his head back as he came hard with a groan that he couldn't hold in. His hips jerked, and he fucked into his fist as he pulsed and spilled over his hand and onto his stomach. As he squeezed out the last few drops, he turned his head sideways and grinned. "Oh yeah, that was awesome."

Mac was staring at him. His brown eyes were even darker than usual and his cheeks were flushed. As Jez stared back, Mac's gaze dropped to Jez's cock. Jez was still stroking himself idly, teasing out the last shivers of pleasure. Mac's breathing sounded ragged as his hand moved fast. He bit his lip, still staring at Jez's dick that was barely softening thanks to Mac's attention.

Jez kept his hand moving, even though the sensation was almost too much. But Mac was clearly getting off on watching him, and that was as hot as fuck.

"Yeah, come on, man. Do it." The words left his lips before he thought about how they sounded.

Jez flamed with a full-body flush as soon as he realised what he'd said, but Mac didn't seem to care.

"I'm gonna—" he gasped and then came, his eyes squeezing shut as though looking at Jez was almost too much to bear.

Jez drew in a shaky breath. Tinny moans and panting from the laptop screen were loud in the otherwise silent room. He leaned forward and closed the lid with his clean hand and then reached for the tissues by his bed. Mac didn't move, and when Jez turned to offer him the box, Mac's eyes were still shut, and he was biting his bottom lip.

Jez nudged him. "Want some tissues?"

Mac snapped his eyes open. He flushed deeper as he avoided Jez's eyes, taking a couple of tissues with a muttered "Thanks."

Jez sighed. This had been really hot, but it would ruin it if Mac bolted and spent the next week ignoring him again.

"You okay?" he asked when they'd both cleaned up a little and rearranged their clothes.

"I guess." Mac's brow furrowed. He shrugged. "This is a bit.... I dunno. It's freaking me out a little."

"It's fun, though, right?" Jez needed to hear Mac admit it. "There's no harm in it."

"Yeah. But I'm not gay."

"I know." Mac was popular with girls. With his height, his broad shoulders, and his sweet smile, they fell over themselves to talk to him. Jez had seen Mac with the ladies, and Mac didn't strike him as someone who was faking it. But it was the same for Jez. Just because he could enjoy getting off with a guy didn't mean he didn't enjoy sleeping with women too. Jez wasn't a big believer in labels. He might be bisexual—not that he'd had much chance to find out—but he didn't want to admit that to Mac in case it freaked him out. "So you've never done anything like this before?"

Mac shook his head. "Nope."

"But you liked it." It wasn't a question, and Mac didn't answer. He didn't need to—it had been obvious. That Mac wasn't comfortable with liking it was also evident.

"Yeah." Mac smiled at last, the slow spread of his grin chasing the worry away from his features. "Yeah, I did."

Chapter Four

Life went on as usual for a couple of weeks. Nothing else happened between them, and neither of them brought it up. But Jez thought about it a lot—when he was wanking, of course, but at other times too.

The days rolled by filled with lectures and tutorials, studying, Jez's occasional shifts at the café, downtime in the evenings, and sleep.

Jez and Mac spent a lot of time hanging out together when they were in the house, even more than they'd done before. He supposed it was because they were the ones who spent the most time at home, and they enjoyed each other's company. Jez preferred chilling out with Mac—playing video games or watching TV—to sitting alone in his room. Staying in rather than going out in the evenings felt normal now, and Jez didn't miss the partying. His overdraft was slowly shrinking, and that was a good feeling too—especially because his dad kept emailing him to ask about his finances. Jez was glad to be able to report that things were heading in the right direction. The lecture about responsibility and entitlement that his dad had given Jez back at the end of the summer term still made Jez ashamed when he thought about it.

Jez and Mac started studying together regularly. Mac was struggling to meet deadlines and worrying about his grades, and Jez was happy to help him. It wasn't that Mac was stupid or not putting the hours in. He did all the required reading and then some, and he had a lot of knowledge, but he always found their written assignments a challenge.

"You make it look so easy," Mac said one night. They were sitting side-by-side on the double bed in Jez's room with their laptops on their knees and a ton of books and papers spread out between them. Mac huffed in frustration. "I've always hated writing essays. I should have picked a subject that doesn't involve putting so many words onto paper."

"What's the problem?"

"I don't know. I feel like I have plenty to say, but I don't know how to get it across coherently."

Jez remembered feeling the same at the start of sixth form at school, but he'd been lucky enough to have a teacher that year who'd helped him a lot with planning and organising his written work.

"Want me to take a look at what you've got so far?"

Mac passed his laptop across and then gave Jez his written notes too. Jez set his nearly finished essay aside and spent the next hour going over Mac's, while Mac listened to his suggestions and chipped in with his own. By the time he'd finished, Mac had a solid outline and seemed much happier, and Jez had gleaned a few new insights from Mac that he wanted to go back and incorporate into his own work, so it was win-win.

"Thanks," Mac said at the end of the evening. "That was really helpful. I never got my head around how to structure an essay properly before. Breaking it down like that was useful."

"You're welcome."

"I want to do better this year. I was gutted last year when I nearly failed my exams."

"Were your parents pissed off with you too?" Jez imagined his own father's reaction if he'd fucked up his exams as well as his finances, and he shuddered at the thought.

Mac snorted, but it wasn't a sound of amusement. "Nope. My dad just said 'I told you so.' He never wanted me to go to uni in the first place. He thinks getting a degree is a waste of time and money. He wanted me to leave school at sixteen and go and work for him. He says there's no jobs for graduates these days, but people always need their roof mended or their house extended. Maybe he's got a point, though."

"Yeah, but...." Jez didn't know what to say. His parents were the opposite. Everyone in Jez's family was a graduate, and it was always expected that Jez would follow in their footsteps—although his father would rather he'd studied medicine or law than geography.

"I want to be a teacher—at secondary school," Mac said. "Mum's on my side, but she doesn't like to argue with Dad."

"That's cool." Jez could imagine Mac as a teacher. He obviously loved the subject, and he had a quiet patience about him that would probably stand him in good stead with difficult kids. "I think you'll make a good one."

A pleased smile spread over Mac's face, and his ears turned pink. "Thanks."

The next time they jerked off together, it was Mac's suggestion. Jez had held off, not wanting to push, but he'd hoped for more between them. It felt like unfinished business.

In the evenings when they weren't studying, they spent a lot of time watching TV or engaging in epic *Mario Kart* battles that went on for hours. It was during one of these that Mac said out of the blue, "Fancy a wank?" He held Jez's gaze, and his expression was challenging, almost as if this was a game too.

Jez tried to hold back a smile. He lost the battle and grinned. "Sure. My place or yours? Or here?" he added as an afterthought.

Mac chuckled. "There's no porn in here. Mine this time?"

It crossed Jez's mind that porn wasn't a requirement. He recalled that last time, when they'd been far too busy looking at each other's dicks to notice the porn, but he didn't think Mac was ready to have that pointed out to him — he was currently inhabiting the village of Denial: population Big Mac. Still, he seemed comfortable there, and Jez wasn't going to be the one to ruin it for him.

Mac's room was tidier than Jez's. His desk was organised neatly rather than being a chaotic mess of books and papers, and his bed was made. The room smelled of Mac, of that woodsy scent of his skin that Jez noticed whenever he was close enough to catch it.

Jez flopped down on Mac's bed, not waiting for an invitation, and he slid his hand down the front of his waistband and started tugging himself into hardness while Mac got his laptop set up between them.

"Impatient?" Mac quirked an eyebrow.

"Horny. It's been a couple of days."

"Bet you come first, then."

"It's not a competition." Jez rolled his eyes. "Unless you want to play the soggy biscuit game."

Mac laughed. "Ew, no thanks."

It was less awkward this time, maybe because of the joking around or because it was becoming familiar, but Jez was more able to let go and stop worrying about what Mac was thinking. Mac wouldn't have asked Jez to do this with him if he hadn't wanted it, so he was clearly into this. Once again, Jez was oblivious to the video—afterwards he couldn't have even said what the couple looked like. He watched Mac instead, focusing on Mac's hand and his cock and the way his breathing got faster as he got close. Jez wondered if Mac was watching him too, and when he glanced up to check, he found he was.

Jez bit back a chuckle. This was so fucked-up, but he didn't care because it was awesome too. These sessions with Mac were hands down the hottest thing he'd ever done with another person, and they hadn't even touched each other. He watched Mac's hand again and imagined those strong fingers wrapped around his own dick, and that was all it took. Jez came, dimly aware of Mac moaning beside him, coming too.

"It was a draw," Jez said.

"Bollocks. You came first."

"By about two seconds."

"Still counts."

"Fuck you." Jez shoulder checked Mac, making him yelp. "Got any tissues?"

"Only bog roll. I'm not as classy as you." Mac passed him a roll of toilet paper from beside the bed. "Wanna go back down and play more Mario Kart?" he asked once they'd cleaned up.

"Sure. But just so you know… you're going down."

"Bring it."

After that, wanking together became a regular thing over the next couple of weeks. Not only at the weekends when they'd been drinking, but a few times a week—basically whenever they could get away and be alone together without it being obvious that something was going on. Sometimes Mac would instigate it, sometimes Jez, but after a few more sessions it got so that they both knew how it would end if they were hanging out together. The tension would thicken, and they'd start catching each other's eye until finally one of them would crack.

They hadn't discussed their little arrangement again since the second time, and they still watched porn—making a point of getting out the laptop in whoever's room they were in and choosing something to watch. But they both knew that they really watched each other, and Jez had given up even trying to hide his interest. He was totally hot for Mac, and watching him get off pushed all Jez's buttons. As for Mac—Jez had no idea what was going on in his head, and Mac didn't seem keen to talk about it. If he was as straight as he claimed, maybe he was into the whole exhibitionist-slash-voyeur vibe they had going on? But Jez didn't care what his motivations were, as long as they could keep doing it.

Chapter Five

When things changed again, alcohol was involved.

It was a Saturday night in the middle of November. Dani was away visiting her boyfriend again, and Josh had gone out early with barely a word to the rest of them. Shawn and Mike tried and failed to persuade Mac and Jez to join them in the student union bar. They'd not told Shawn and Mike about their staying-in pact. It wasn't worth the hassle because it would only have made Shawn more determined to lead them astray. They'd stuck with their excuses of finances and studying respectively. Both were still true, after all.

"Just come out for a few beers," Shawn said. "You two are like an old married couple, for fuck's sake. All you do is hang out together and watch TV."

"Sometimes we study," Mac said.

"And play video games," Jez added. They were currently in the middle of a *Super Smash Bros.* battle. Jez's cheeks heated at the "married couple" dig. He didn't dare look at Mac to see if he'd reacted too.

"Like that's any better. And Mac, Maria was asking after you last weekend, and she's gonna be there tonight. I reckon you're well in there. Why stay in and jerk off when you could be out with a hot babe like her?"

Mac stiffened beside Jez. His onscreen character froze, just like he did, and Jez took the opportunity to attack, kicking him off the platform.

"Loser." Jez nudged Mac in the ribs, trying to distract him. Shawn's dig was a little close for comfort.

"Nah. I'm not that into her," Mac finally said.

"But she's gorgeous!" Shawn sounded like a man who knew he was fighting a losing battle.

"Not tonight."

Jez couldn't help feeling glad that Mac would rather stay in with him, even though he told himself it didn't mean anything.

After the others had gone, they carried on playing for a couple of hours. They were drinking snakebite this weekend — strong lager mixed with equally strong cider — and Jez's coordination was affected. He was more pissed than he had been in ages.

"You fucker!" he cursed as Mac sent his character flying off the platform again to win the best of three. Jez tossed his controller aside and threw himself back against the sofa cushions. "I'm done."

"Are you rage quitting? That's always the sign of a sore loser." But Mac set his controller down too, turned the game off, and settled back beside him.

"If I carry on any longer, I'll end up playing it in my sleep all night." Jez yawned. The alcohol had made him sleepy and relaxed, but he wasn't ready to go to bed yet. With the house to themselves and Mac's knee bumping his, Jez's mind turned to other things they could be doing, and his body started to respond. He was like one of Pavlov's dogs around Mac now, only horny instead of hungry. Just looking at him made Jez want to get off.

Mac didn't reply immediately. Jez wondered if Mac was thinking the same thing he was. Sometimes it felt like a game of chicken as they waited to see who'd make the first move.

Mac shifted slightly, moving his hand to cover the bulge in his jeans. Jez didn't react, but his eyes followed the movement, a thrum of arousal zinging through him as Mac started to stroke himself idly through the fabric.

"You wanna?" Mac asked, his voice a little rough already.

"I guess." The rasp in Jez's voice gave him away in his attempt at sounding casual.

Mac stood and offered his hand to Jez.

Jez paused for a split second before taking it and letting Mac pull him up. The warm brush of his palm against Jez's was electric, and Jez's head was suddenly full of other places that Mac's hands could touch him — if only Mac wanted to.

Pushing those traitorous thoughts aside, he dropped Mac's hand as though it burned and followed him up the stairs.

"Your room?" Mac paused with his hand on the door handle — Jez's was closest to the top of the stairs.

"Sure."

There was nothing awkward about this now. After the past few weeks, they knew exactly how this would go. Mac made himself comfortable on Jez's bed while Jez got his laptop. By the time Jez sat down, Mac had already pushed his clothing down enough to get his cock out and was stroking himself slowly.

"Starting without me?" Jez asked.

"Yep. I'm horny. Gonna take a while, though, after all the booze."

"Yeah. Me too." Jez thought maybe that wasn't a bad thing. When they were sober, they both came pretty fast. It was hot but rather clinical. But when they were both a bit drunk, it was usually a more leisurely affair, and Jez liked it when it lasted a little longer.

Jez pulled up his bookmarks. He intended to click on one they'd watched before that they both liked, but he must have accidentally hit the wrong link because instead of the usual girl-guy combination, the video that started playing as Jez unzipped his jeans had two guys on a sofa with a girl between them. The girl kissed first one guy and then the other with deep dirty kisses.

"Oops, sorry." Jez's face heated. "I didn't mean to open that one. Let me find something else."

"No, it's fine. Two guys doing one girl—that's kinda hot."

"Yeah, but…." Jez squirmed with embarrassment as he tried to find the words to explain why this was a bad idea. Then the guys on the screen helped him out by leaning across the girl and kissing each other while she looked on, smiling and encouraging them.

"Oh." Mac's hand stilled.

"Yeah. It's not so much two guys doing one girl as all of them doing each other… in various ways and combinations." Jez leaned forward to reach the laptop, but Mac stopped him with a firm grip to his wrist.

"Leave it."

Jez swallowed hard, nerves and arousal combining to rocket his heart rate up. "If you're sure?"

"I'm sure."

"Okay, then."

They watched in silence. Mac seemed to forget about his dick at first, watching the action on the screen intently. Jez sneaked a look and saw that Mac's erection had flagged a bit, probably been scared away by all the gay that was happening in front of him right now. But Mac was still watching nevertheless. Jez had no idea why he wanted to. As far as he knew, Mac didn't have a bi-curious bone — or *boner* — in his body, he thought, and then tried not to laugh out loud at his own bad joke.

As the video progressed, Jez stopped worrying about Mac and started to get into it. He'd bookmarked this for a reason. One of the guys was tall, built, and dark like Mac, and the other was a little smaller, leaner, and had messy dirty-blond hair like Jez did. The girl was gorgeous too, a redhead who was into the whole guy-on-guy thing, and frankly the whole video was hot as fuck.

They'd moved on from making out, and the girl was sucking each of the guys' dicks in turn, switching between them and making appreciative noises. Jez gripped his cock and squeezed because he knew what was coming. Sure enough, the trio on the screen switched positions. The dark guy lay on his back while the girl sat on his face, and the blond guy kneeled over the dark guy's body and swallowed his dick down like he hadn't eaten for a week.

Fuck.

Jez glanced at Mac again. His hand was moving faster now, and he was utterly transfixed by the video, not looking at Jez this time, and his breathing was fast. He was obviously really turned on by this, and that was what gave Jez the courage to finally suggest something he'd been thinking about ever since the first time they'd jerked off together.

"I'll suck you off if you want?"

Mac snapped his head around to stare at Jez. Their faces were close, close enough that it would be easy for Jez to lean in and lick at Mac's bitten lips, push his tongue between them, and taste him. He didn't think Mac would let him do that, but maybe he'd let Jez suck his cock? Letting someone else get you off wasn't gay. Jez could be a convenient mouth, and he was okay with that—more than okay, in fact. He wanted it badly.

Mac swallowed hard, and his eyes were elderberry dark as he pinned Jez with them. "You want to?"

Jez nodded. "Wouldn't have offered if I didn't."

There was a long pause punctuated only by moans and wet sounds coming from the laptop.

"Okay," Mac finally answered. His voice was barely more than a whisper.

Without giving Mac a chance to change his mind, Jez moved. Careful not to dislodge the laptop where it lay between them, he climbed over Mac to kneel astride his legs and lowered his face into Mac's groin.

Mac was still gripping his cock, so Jez nuzzled his balls instead where they bulged out of his fly, breathing him in. He smelled unmistakably masculine, and it made Jez's cock throb. Jez licked, and Mac's breath caught. Jez licked again, pressing open-mouthed kisses to the wrinkled skin of Mac's sac. He brought his hand up and pushed Mac's away so that he could curl his fingers around Mac's cock. *God*, Mac was thick, and he felt amazing in Jez's hand. Jez licked slowly up the underside of Mac's shaft, and when he reached the head, he sucked him in, tasting musk, salt, and sweetness that made his mouth water.

Mac didn't move, but he made a small noise, somewhere between a huff of breath and a moan. Jez took him deeper, trying to coax more sounds out of him with his lips and tongue. It had been years since Jez had done this for another guy, but during that term when he'd swapped blowjobs with his roommate, he'd got pretty good at it. He supposed it was like riding a bicycle. The sensation of a cock in his mouth was familiar, and Jez had forgotten how much he enjoyed taking another guy apart like this — or maybe he'd never wanted to admit how much he liked it before.

It didn't take Jez long to get into a rhythm. He went deliberately slowly, wanting to tease and make Mac last. Mac hadn't made a sound since Jez first started sucking, and he'd clenched his hands tight by his sides as though he was afraid to touch. Jez could almost feel the fear and uncertainty rolling off him along with the intense arousal, and he sympathised. He remembered how that felt, wanting it so much but being ashamed of it at the same time.

He pulled off for a moment, fisting Mac's cock in his hand instead and glanced up. "Is this okay? I can stop if you want."

Mac's cheeks were flushed, his lips pink. He looked wrecked, and he hadn't even come yet.

"No. Please…. It's good."

Jez smiled. "Okay."

Mac slowly relaxed. He let his hands uncurl and eventually put a tentative palm on Jez's shoulder. Jez made an encouraging sound and Mac moved his hand into Jez's hair, sliding his fingers into the tangled strands. He grunted as Jez licked around the head before taking him deep again. Jez couldn't manage all of Mac's length but it was fun trying. His jaw was starting to ache now, so he sped things up a little. His own cock hung heavy and aching out of his fly. He'd have liked to get a hand to it, but he was using one to prop himself up and had wrapped the other around the bit of Mac's cock he couldn't take. Mac must be close now, though, and then Jez could jerk off. It wouldn't take much—Jez was so turned on by this.

Mac flexed his hips, and his cock bumped the back of Jez's throat. "I'm close," he gasped.

Jez considered pulling off, but then thought *fuck it*. He hadn't minded swallowing back in the day, so he carried on sucking.

Mac came with a hoarse moan, and he tightened his hand in Jez's hair, holding him down as Mac's cock pulsed and filled his mouth with come. Jez gagged as the head of Mac's cock hit the back of his throat again.

"Fuck. Sorry." Mac took his hand away abruptly, putting it on Jez's shoulder as Jez drew back, wiping his mouth as he swallowed.

"It's okay." Jez hadn't minded. The shattering of Mac's control was fucking hot and more than worth the discomfort. "You took me by surprise, that's all." Jez sat back on his heels, and Mac's gaze slid down to his dick. Rock-hard and dripping, pointing right at Mac.

Mac stared at it like it was a snake about to bite him. "I, uh.... Did you want me to—?"

"You don't have to." Jez couldn't help the twinge of disappointment, even though he'd known there was no way that Mac was going to want to suck his dick in return. He climbed over Mac and lay back down in his previous spot. "But I'm gonna finish myself off now if that's all right with you?" The video had ended, but Jez didn't need it, not with his imagination, and the taste of Mac still on his tongue. If this made Mac uncomfortable, that was too bad. A little discomfort was a small price to pay for an awesome blowjob, and Mac didn't have to watch. Jez hitched his T-shirt up and then breathed in sharply as he curled his fingers around his neglected cock.

But Mac surprised him by shuffling down the bed after pulling his trousers back up. He lay on his side and put his large hand on Jez's thigh, then slid it up to wrap it around Jez's hand where he was stroking himself. "Let me."

Hell yes. Jez would settle for a hand job. It was more than he'd hoped for.

Mac didn't touch him apart from the hand on Jez's cock, but Jez could feel the warmth of his body in the space between them. Their heads were almost touching, and Mac's breath whispered across Jez's cheek. Mac was hesitant at first, moving his hand too slowly. But then he seemed to get more confident, and Jez encouraged him when he got the speed and pressure just right.

"Yeah, like that." Jez's voice came out hoarse and strained. "Fuck."

It was over way too soon. Jez wanted to make the most of the experience. Who knew if Mac would ever touch his dick again? But he was too turned on. This whole fucked-up situation was too hot, and Jez couldn't hold out.

Pleasure tore through him, and he went taut as he came with a gasp. White sticky streaks patterned his clenched abs as Mac kept stroking him until Jez's cock gave a final spurt and he relaxed, sated. He gently pushed Mac's hand away. "'S too much now."

Jez grabbed some tissues from beside the bed and cleaned himself up with Mac lying silently beside him. When Jez was clean and decent again, he turned his head. Mac met his gaze and gave a small smile that didn't reach his eyes. He looked uncertain, anxious, and Jez expected him to make his excuses and leave quickly. But he didn't.

"Have you done that before?" Mac asked.

Jez assumed he was talking about the blowjob. "Not since school, but yeah." His stomach fluttered with nerves. He hadn't admitted that to any of his new friends since leaving school. As far as all his uni friends were concerned, Jez was 100 percent straight.

"You're good at it." Mac flushed, but he didn't look away.

"Thanks... I guess?" Jez gave a small smile. "I had a bit of practice. But it's not that hard." He cleared his throat and swallowed; the bitter taste of Mac's come still lingered.

"But—" Mac frowned. "—You're not gay, are you?"

Jez shook his head. "Nah. I like girls, but I suppose I like guys too—some guys, anyway." His heart beat faster as he waited for Mac's reaction. It wasn't exactly a declaration, but surely Mac would get the implied meaning and realise what Jez was saying even though he didn't dare say the words out loud.

Mac's frown softened slightly, but he still looked puzzled. "This is doing my head in a bit, to be honest," he admitted. "I've never wanted to touch a guy before. I've always fancied girls, slept with girls, thought about girls. And now...."

Now what? Jez wanted to ask. But he was afraid to push, so instead he shrugged. "Don't beat yourself up over it. It felt good, what we just did, yeah?" Mac nodded. "So don't overthink it. It's a bit of fun. Two mates helping each other out. It doesn't make you gay. It doesn't even make you bi. Think of it as prison sex." He forced a grin, trying to make a joke of it, but his stomach twisted unhappily as he added, "You're simply making do with what's available."

Mac huffed out a quiet chuckle at that. He didn't deny it, but Jez was sure he could see genuine affection in Mac's expression, and that was good enough for Jez. This was only ever going to be a temporary thing. Sooner or later Mac would meet another girl and Jez would be firmly back in the friend zone, remembered only as a phase, a weird aberration in Mac's sexual history.

Chapter Six

After the first blowjob, the rules changed. Hands-off became very definitely hands-on—and sometimes mouth in Jez's case. Mac made no move to reciprocate by blowing Jez, but he was always good for a hand job. Jez was really into sucking Mac's cock, but his favourite thing they did now was to jerk each other off at the same time. They tried it sitting side-by-side, but it was way too awkward, and lying on their sides face-to-face worked better. They couldn't see whatever porn they were supposedly watching then, but Jez didn't care at all, and Mac didn't seem to miss it either. Jez loved the intimacy of that position, the way their breath mingled and their knees bumped. They usually took off their T-shirts to save on laundry, and the sight of Mac's broad muscled chest and the overpowering scent of his skin usually had Jez coming embarrassingly fast.

He was stuck in a weird no man's land with Mac. They were friends who got each other off, but aside from that, they didn't touch, and kissing was out of the question. Jez assumed it was, anyway—there was no way he was going to try it, or broach the subject. He had a feeling that kissing another guy would be a hard limit for Mac. Jez had never kissed another guy either. He'd never wanted to before, but now he found himself thinking about it all the time, and not only when they were jerking each other off, but whenever Mac smiled at him in a certain way, or made him laugh, or caught his eye across the living room when the others were around.

Mac was in Jez's room one evening, sitting on Jez's bed, working on their latest assignment, when Jez's phone rang. He looked at the screen. "It's my parents."

"Want me to go?"

"No, it's fine. I'll try and be quick." They had all their work spread out in here and it would be a hassle for Mac to move rooms.

Jez pressed the button to take the call, wondering which parent it would be. "Hi."

"Hi, darling." It was his mum. "I thought I'd call as we haven't heard from you for a week or so. How are you?"

"Okay, thanks."

They chatted for a few minutes. Jez didn't have much news, but he reassured her that he was managing to keep up with his studying despite his part-time job. "I only do two shifts a week, one at the weekend and one evening. It's not interfering with uni at all."

"And are you eating okay?" she pressed. "I don't want you starving yourself to save money for going out."

"Mum, I'm fine. I'm managing my money better this year, and I'm hardly going out at all. I'm eating fine." He caught Mac looking at him. Mac grinned, and Jez rolled his eyes.

"I wish your father hadn't insisted." She lowered her voice. "You know I thought we should pay off the overdraft for you, you could always pay us back once you're working. But you know what he's like—"

"It's fine, Mum." Jez cut her off. They'd been through this enough in the summer; he didn't need to hear it again. "Anyway, you caught me in the middle of an assignment, so I should probably get back to it."

"Hang on, your dad wants to talk to you too. Let me get him." There was a rustle, and her voice was distant and muffled as she called, "Martin!" Then, back to normal, she said, "Okay, here he is. Now take care, darling, and stay in touch, please. You can always email me if you don't want to phone. Bye for now."

Jez's shoulders stiffened instinctively as he waited for his dad to come on the line. He should get into the habit of emailing them more often, and maybe then he wouldn't have to put up with the awkward phone calls. He didn't mind talking to his mum, but his dad always got his back up.

"Hello, Jeremy." His father's voice boomed down the line. "How are your grades this term?"

Jez gritted his teeth. Would it kill his dad to ask him in a more general way how he was before quizzing him about his performance? But he schooled his voice into politeness as he answered his dad's questions about his course and then, inevitably, about his finances. He was very aware of Mac listening in, even though Mac wasn't watching him — he had a notebook open and a pen in his hand, but he was doodling rather than writing.

Once his dad was reassured that Jez was working hard and not pissing all his money away on beer, he finally said in a more congenial tone, "And you're okay? Everything all right generally?"

"Yeah. I'm fine, Dad, thanks. But I have to go now. I have an assignment to finish." Those were the magic words. No way would his dad keep him from studying.

"Oh, okay. I won't keep you, then. Take care."

"Bye, Dad."

"Bye."

Jez disconnected the call with a sigh. "Ugh." He dropped his head back against the wall with a thud.

"Your dad's pretty hard on you, huh?" Mac said.

"Yeah. He was livid with me last year for getting into debt."

Mac frowned. "If you don't mind me asking… they only give you a very basic allowance, yeah? I was wondering why. I mean… your dad's a doctor, isn't he? And your mum…. What does she do again?"

"Solicitor."

"They can't be short of money. So how come they don't help you out more?"

Jez shrugged. "It's just the way my dad is. He says I need to be independent and learn to manage my money. He comes from a working class background, and he had to work bloody hard to get where he is today. Dad doesn't want me to be one of those entitled kids who expects a free ride from their parents. It's fair enough, really. But I wish he didn't make me feel so bad about it. I fucked up last year and I know it. But I hate feeling like I'm disappointing him."

"Well, you're back on track now, yeah?" Mac's eyes were warm and reassuring.

"Yeah." Jez smiled. Sometimes he couldn't help smiling when he looked at Mac. "Yeah, I am."

One afternoon Jez got back to the house after a tutorial that finished early and found Josh in the kitchen making instant coffee.

"Want anything?" Josh asked. "There's enough hot water."

"Yeah, I'll have a coffee too, cheers. White, no sugar."

"The opposite of mine, then." Josh grinned.

Jez watched as Josh spooned and stirred, adding milk to Jez's and two heaped teaspoonfuls of sugar to the dark liquid in his own mug.

They took their coffees into the living room. Josh sat on one of the sofas and picked up a magazine. Jez took the other sofa, sitting with his elbows on his knees and staring at the carpet as he listened to the sound of the pages rustle as Josh turned them, obviously searching for something that caught his interest.

Jez felt a question he'd been wanting to ask Josh for ages itching at the back of his mind. He sighed and shifted in his seat, picking at the skin around his fingers as he tried to work up the courage.

He finally asked, the words coming out in a rush, "When did you know you were gay?"

The sound of the pages turning stopped, and there was a long silence. When Jez finally dared to look up, Josh was watching him with a thoughtful expression. Jez was relieved to see there wasn't a trace of teasing there, but he felt his cheeks heat anyway.

"I dunno. Always, maybe? There wasn't a big sudden 'oh my God, I'm gay' moment for me. I always had crushes on boys, and when I worked out what my dick was for, I didn't want to put it in girls. So it was pretty obvious."

"So, you've never…?"

"I tried it once." Josh wrinkled his nose and chuckled. "But I couldn't get it up, so that only made me more sure." There was a long pause, and for a moment Jez thought he might have got away without having to talk about himself. But Josh held his gaze, and his green eyes were curious.

"Why do you want to know?"

Jez winced inwardly. But if he didn't want to talk about it, he shouldn't have brought it up in the first place. "I, um…." He took a deep breath. "I think I like guys. But I like girls too, so I didn't take the liking-blokes part seriously before."

"Before what?"

Jez floundered for a moment. No way was he going to mention Mac's part in his realisations. "Nothing specific. I've just been thinking about it a lot recently—and watching gay porn." That part was true, and it had been very enlightening.

Josh's lips curved in a knowing smile, and his lip ring glinted where it caught the light. "Is this the bit where you ask if you can test out the theory with me? Because I would—if you wanted to."

Jez gaped in shock, because that absolutely *wasn't* what he was suggesting, but he let himself imagine it for a split second. It would be straightforward with Josh. He was attractive, there would be no complicated feelings, and Jez would be with someone who knew what he was doing and was into it 100 percent—physically, at least. It would be the perfect way to test out his newfound interest in men and maybe to experiment with some of the things Jez wanted to try but didn't dare suggest to Mac. But no…. Jez felt a strange sense of loyalty to Mac even though it was totally misplaced. He didn't for a moment think that Mac would care about him fooling around with someone else, but it didn't feel right. Plus having sex with one housemate was awkward enough; the last thing Jez needed was to make his life even more complicated.

"No. That's not what this conversation was about. But... thanks for the offer, really."

"Any time." Josh grinned. "Deflowering gay virgins is fun."

"Fuck off." Jez snorted. "I'm not completely innocent."

"Oh yeah?" Josh looked gleeful at the potential for gossip.

Jez ignored him and picked up his coffee, taking a gulp to stop himself from oversharing. It was tempting to spill everything to Josh, but Jez couldn't risk it. Not when the secret belonged to Mac as well as him.

When it was obvious that no more juicy details were forthcoming, Josh picked up his magazine again and went back to reading.

Jez finished his coffee in silence, but his thoughts were deafening.

Chapter Seven

In late November it was Shawn's birthday. There was no way Jez and Mac could get away with staying in when all their mates were going out to help Shawn celebrate, so they invoked the special occasion clause in their pact and agreed to join the others for once.

It felt weird getting ready to go out after so many nights in. They were going clubbing, but there was no dress code; casual would be fine. Even so, Jez made more effort with his appearance than he had done in months. He showered and dressed in his best jeans and a black T-shirt that hugged his torso and emphasised his narrow waist and wide shoulders. His shaggy, dirty-blond hair didn't need much styling, so he just combed a little wax through it to keep it from going fluffy. He stared in the mirror critically. *Not bad*. He tilted his face so the light caught the golden brown stubble on his jaw. Yeah. He'd do.

Jez went down to the living room where a whole gang of people was hanging out. As well as his housemates there were also several other friends of Shawn's, most of whom Jez had met before. They were all getting stuck into the booze—preloading to save money on overpriced beers in the pubs and clubs they'd be hitting later. There were a ton of bottles on the coffee table, beer, wine, and cheap brands of vodka and whisky, and various mixers. Upbeat music poured out of the speakers, and Jez felt a thrill of excitement. He'd got used to staying in, but tonight was going to be fun. Being a hermit had its downside.

Judging by the loud conversation and raucous laughter, he had some catching up to do on the alcohol front. He made his way to the table and poured himself a vodka and coke—light on the coke, heavy on the vodka. He took a swig and felt the burn of the alcohol all the way to his stomach.

"Jez, my man!" A heavy hand clapped on his shoulder, and he turned to see Shawn, flushed and clearly pissed already. Knowing Shawn, he'd probably started at lunchtime. "You're coming out later, yeah?"

"Yeah. Gotta help you celebrate no longer being a teenager, haven't I?" Jez raised his glass, and Shawn bumped it erratically with the can of Special Brew he was holding.

"Too fucking right, mate. 'Bout time you and that pussy Mac came out and got some action. You've been joined at the hip for weeks. People are starting to wonder about your bromance, you know."

Jez's stomach lurched but he schooled his features into amused indifference. He scanned the room quickly for Mac to see if he was listening. Sure enough, Mac was watching their exchange from the sofa, and he wasn't doing a good job of hiding his discomfort. His jaw was tense as he glared at Shawn.

Jez decided to front it out, but he kept his tone light. "Don't be a dick, Shawny. You know we've had our reasons for staying in this term. Anyway, we're coming out tonight. Wouldn't miss it."

But Shawn frowned, drunk and aggressive. "I should hope so. I'm not having you staying in on my birthday. That would be so fucking gay."

Jez's body tensed at the word. Shawn didn't mean it literally. It was one of those things people said—a stupid insult that Jez had probably thrown out himself hundreds of times over the years. But now it made his palms sweat and his heart pound with the irrational fear that somehow Shawn *knew*.

Jez caught Mac's eye for a split second before looking back at Shawn's stupid, belligerent face. Mac appeared as stunned as Jez felt, so he was clearly going to be no help here. Jez tried to find the right response, afraid he'd say the wrong thing or give them away by his expression or the tone of his voice. But before he could gather his wits and find some words, distraction came from an unexpected quarter.

"Staying in isn't *gay*, Shawn," Josh drawled from behind Shawn. "We've been through this. Will you please stop with using that as an insult for everything? As the resident gay, I'm getting tired of hearing it."

Shawn flushed. "It's just an expression," he muttered, but at least he had the grace to look guilty.

"Well, it's a stupid one." Josh's eyes narrowed as if daring Shawn to argue more.

There was an awkward pause. Jez was suddenly aware that the chatter had died down. Most people in the room seemed to be listening to their little exchange.

"Which pub are we going to later?" Jez wanted to get the conversation away from dangerous ground.

Luckily Shawn took the bait, and the moment passed. Josh gave Jez a quick wink before turning away to talk to Dani again.

When Jez dared look back at Mac a little later, he seemed to have relaxed and was deep in conversation with a blonde girl Jez hadn't seen before. She was pretty, and she kept giggling at things Mac said and twirling her hair. Jez ignored the unpleasant lurch of discomfort in his gut. Mac could flirt with anyone he wanted; it wasn't Jez's business.

In the pub, the girl—Gemma, Jez found out when Mac introduced them—was still hanging around Mac. It didn't make Jez feel any better when it turned out that Gemma was not only pretty but also funny and intelligent. She was studying Politics and Philosophy and had opinions on everything. In other circumstances Jez would probably have been attracted to her and tried to get her attention for himself, but tonight he was uneasy and unsettled, and he was struggling to follow the conversation because his own thoughts were too distracting.

He excused himself to go to the bar. It was busy, but it didn't take too long to get served as they had lots of people working. As the barman was pouring Jez's pint, a girl squeezed in beside Jez, digging him in the ribs with an elbow.

"Oops, sorry," she said. "But when you're my height, you have to be pushy." She couldn't have been much over five feet tall and looked like a little pixie with spiky hair in an unnatural shade of red, big dark eyes, and an upturned nose.

"I can only imagine." Jez was six foot now and had had his growth spurt at thirteen. He couldn't remember being that small.

She grinned. "Yeah, it's okay for you."

She spoke with a slight accent. Jez tried to place it—Italian, maybe?

The barman returned with Jez's pint. "Anything else?" he asked.

"Oh, could you get me a pint of Dry Blackthorn if you're already being served?" the girl asked. "Here's the money." She put a pile of coins down on the bar. Jez would have offered to pay for hers, but she pushed them towards him insistently.

The barman went off to pour her drink.

"I'm Gabi, by the way. You're here for Shawn's birthday too, yes?"

"Yes." Jez nodded. "I'm Jez."

"Cool."

When they both had their drinks, Gabi joined Jez's group, squeezing in beside him on the bench seat. He introduced her to Mac, and she already knew Gemma. Mac caught Jez's eye and gave a slight grin and eyebrow raise, maybe in encouragement.

As the evening progressed, the girls stuck with them. Jez was enjoying Gabi's company. She was fun to talk to and cute to look at. She wasn't hiding her interest, and normally Jez would have gone for it and flirted right back, but tonight he was distracted by what was going on with Mac and Gemma. He found himself listening in to their conversation instead of paying attention to Gabi. A rising unease tightened his chest and made his gut clench. Jez was reluctant to admit he was jealous, but deep down he recognised the unfamiliar emotion even though he tried to ignore it. Instead he tried to drown his feelings in beer. If he drank enough, he might manage to stop moping around after his mate and get with the program. Gabi was into him, and she was cool. It had been way too long since he'd hooked up with a girl. Maybe he needed to get back in the saddle.

By the time they got to the club, Jez was well on the way to being drunk but not quite at the sloppy stage. He was buzzed and feeling more chilled, the alcohol temporarily clouding his anxieties. Gabi took his hand and pulled him towards the packed dance floor, and he followed. Once they were lost in the throng, she turned to face him. Pressed close by the crowd, it was easier to dance with his hands on her hips. She put her arms around his neck, tilted her head back, and smiled.

Jez let his gaze roam over the rest of the dancers. Lots of the others from their group had joined them. He caught sight of Shawn with a curly-haired girl, and Josh and Dani dancing together — blatantly dirty dancing in a completely over-the-top way — and then he found who he was looking for. Mac's dark head stood out because he was a couple of inches taller than most other blokes, and sure enough, he was dancing with Gemma. Jez watched as she tossed her hair and looked at Mac seductively from under her lashes. Mac smiled and moved closer. Jez tore his gaze away, an uneasy feeling lodged like stone in the pit of his belly.

"Excuse me." He spoke into Gabi's ear so she'd hear him over the deep bass of the music. "I need to pee."

"Okay." She carried on dancing, unconcerned.

Jez pushed his way through the bodies until he reached the door at the back that led to the toilets. There were two sets of doors between the club and the toilets, and when the inner door swung shut, it was quiet, with the noise from outside almost completely gone. Only one other guy was in there, and Jez joined him at the urinal. He really did need to go; the beer was a heavy weight in his bladder. The other guy zipped up and left, and Jez was aware of someone else coming in behind him. A large figure moved in close beside him, in clear breach of unspoken urinal etiquette. When Jez realised it was Mac, he relaxed.

"All right," Jez greeted him. "Having fun? Gemma seems cool." He tried to keep his tone casual, but he wasn't sure if he managed it. There was a tightness in his throat that lent tension to his voice.

"Uh, yeah. She's great," Mac replied. Jez tried to squash the jealousy that twisted his gut. "What about you and Gabi? Are you gonna go for it? I think she's into you."

Jez glanced sideways, trying to gauge Mac's true feelings, but Mac's face gave nothing away as he stared at the tiled wall.

"Yeah, why not?" Jez replied briskly. "It's about time we got some action, right?" He tucked himself away and went to wash his hands. He looked at the reflection of Mac's back in the mirror. Mac's broad shoulders stretched the fabric of his T-shirt, the bunched muscles visible through the thin material.

When Mac joined Jez at the sinks, he was still avoiding Jez's gaze. Jez took the opportunity to stare, cataloguing the sharp line of Mac's jaw, the shadow of his stubble, and the deep brown pools of his eyes. Jez clenched his teeth in the uncomfortable silence.

As they went back into the main part of the club, the sweaty heat of dancing bodies, the scent of perfume vying with cologne, and the loud pulse of music assaulted Jez's senses. He felt dizzy for a moment, losing his footing slightly as he adjusted to the sudden change from the cool quiet of the toilets. Mac put his hand on Jez's shoulder, the weight of it steadying him.

"You okay, mate?"

"Yeah. Yeah… just a bit too much beer. I'm not used to it."

They found their friends on the dance floor again. Gabi approached Jez as soon as she saw him, a smile on her face and a sway to her hips. He let her take his hands and pull him close. He met Mac's gaze over the top of her head, though, and they stared at each other for a moment before Mac turned away.

Jez lost himself in the rhythm of the music and the sensation of Gabi's body moving with his. The alcohol had dulled his senses but done nothing to ease the discomfort that sat heavy in his chest. But Gabi felt good against him, and even though his heart wasn't in it, his body responded. He let himself fall into the well-practised moves of seduction, holding her close and stroking her back, leaning down so he could press his face into her neck. She smelled as pretty as she looked, floral and sweet, but it wasn't what Jez was craving.

When their lips finally met, it felt inevitable, but all Jez could think about was what it would be like to kiss Mac instead. To have a body larger than his own in his arms, to be leaning up to kiss instead of down. He closed his eyes and pulled Gabi closer, trying to blot out his traitorous thoughts and feeling like an arsehole for not appreciating her.

Jez had no idea how much time passed as they kissed and danced and kissed some more — an hour or so, perhaps? Eventually Gabi pulled his head down and said into his ear, "Do you want to get out of here? You can come back to my place." She drew back and smiled, hopeful.

Decision time.

Jez scanned the dance floor for Mac and saw him, still dancing with Gemma. They weren't kissing yet, but Jez assumed it was only a matter of time.

"Yeah, okay. But I need to go to the toilet again." He didn't really. But he wanted a moment to clear his head; to be sure he was making the right decision.

He brushed past Mac as he went but didn't catch his eye.

He didn't realise Mac had followed him until the door to the toilets slammed shut behind them. Mac had Jez pinned up against the wall before Jez knew what was happening. Mac's face was set, a muscle ticking in his jaw as he glared down at him.

"What the fuck, Mac?" Jez didn't make any move to push him away. His heart was going like a trip hammer, and the scent of Mac's sweat was making him harder in thirty seconds than Gabi's kisses had in an hour.

The crash of Mac's lips against his was the last thing Jez expected. Frozen with shock, his mouth went slack as Mac forced his tongue into Jez's mouth, greedy and demanding. But after a few seconds, Jez's brain caught up with what was happening, and his body followed with a hot surge of arousal. He grabbed Mac's face in both hands and held him there—not that Mac was trying to pull away. It felt like Mac was trying to take up residence in Jez's mouth, and Jez was okay with that. He gave as good as he got, kissing Mac back fiercely, eliciting a groan that went right to Jez's cock.

The sound of the outer door made them spring apart. They gazed at each other for a split second, eyes wide, breath panting, and then Jez ducked around Mac and went to the sink. Having a piss would be a physical impossibility right now, even if raging erections at the urinal were socially acceptable.

Mac headed for a cubicle, and the door clanged shut, followed by the scrape of a bolt.

Fuck, fuck, fuck.

The other bloke who'd come in headed to the urinal. Jez's hands shook as he ran cold water on them and splashed it onto his burning cheeks. He stared at himself in the mirror, taking in his hectic flush and dark pupils that nearly eclipsed the blue of his irises. His cock ached.

Jez waited. The newcomer seemed to take forever to piss while Jez washed his hands slowly.

Finally the other guy left.

"He's gone." Jez's raised voice echoed off the tiles.

No answer.

He tried again. "Are we going to talk about what just happened?"

Mac opened the door, his cheeks as flushed as Jez's, but he met Jez's gaze and held it. "Not here," he said. "Back at home?"

"Now?"

Mac nodded.

Chapter Eight

The walk home was tense. Thankfully they didn't have far to go because it was near to freezing now. They walked quickly. Their breath made clouds of vapour, and the chill stung Jez's cheeks. Dressed for clubbing, they only had thin jackets with no hats, gloves, or scarves. Silence stretched awkwardly between them. Jez had no idea what to say. His stomach was full of rampaging butterflies as he wondered what was going to happen when they got back to the house.

Mac finally asked, "Was Gabi pissed off at you for ditching her?"

"No," Jez said. "But I told her I was feeling sick, so she couldn't argue with that. She gave me her number."

"You gonna use it?"

"I dunno." Jez doubted it. It wouldn't be fair to string her along when he wasn't feeling it. Mac's rough kisses had obliterated all memory of her lips. "What about you and Gemma?"

"Nothing happened between us. She was dancing with Mike when we left, so I didn't bother to say anything."

Back at the house, Jez let them in. He went straight upstairs, and Mac followed him in silence. Jez pushed open the door of his room, and the creak of a floorboard told him that Mac was still behind him. His heart thumped against his ribs, and he felt dizzy with nerves. Jez switched on the bedside lamp and turned. Mac looked huge in the dim light, and the yellow glow softened his features as he met Jez's gaze. He swallowed, the click of his throat audible in the silence.

"What are we doing?" Jez's voice was hoarse.

Mac shrugged, a small movement of his shoulders. "Can I kiss you again?"

Jez huffed a nervous laugh. "You didn't ask the first time."

Mac's lips twitched. "I didn't know I was going to do it till it happened."

"Get over here, then."

This time the kiss was cautious, more like a first kiss than the crazy impulsivity of before. As their lips parted and tongues touched, Jez closed his eyes and let the slow wave of sensation engulf him. Mac's hands cupped his face at first, still chilled from the winter air outside but warming fast. Jez held Mac's waist, tugging him closer until their hips bumped together. God, Mac was hard already, and Jez was getting there fast. He slid his hands lower and palmed Mac's arse, half expecting him to pull away, but he didn't. Instead he groaned into Jez's mouth and kissed him more hungrily. The rasp of his stubble on Jez's was alien and thrilling, and the size and strength of Mac's hands as he slid them up the back of Jez's T-shirt and stroked them over his skin were so different to what Jez was used to. He shivered.

"Sorry, are they cold?" Mac murmured.

"Yeah, but don't stop."

Overwhelmed with arousal and the thrill of finally getting to touch Mac like this, Jez wanted more. He was done being cautious. Mac had started this, and Jez was going to take what he could get while it lasted. He kissed Mac again, hard and deep, and slid his hands up the front of Mac's T-shirt, palming over the ridges of Mac's abs and up to his chest. Mac's skin was smooth, and his nipples hardened under Jez's teasing fingers. Jez stroked and pinched lightly, and Mac whimpered, pressing his hips harder into Jez.

Jez broke the kiss to pull his own T-shirt off, craving skin-on-skin. "Yours too," he demanded.

Mac only hesitated for a second before complying.

They kissed again, and the contact of their warm, bare chests pressing close together made Jez's balls ache with the need to come. *So good, so fucking good.* He grabbed Mac's hips and hauled him closer, grinding their erections together. It was amazing, but it still wasn't enough.

"Come on," he gasped out between kisses, pushing Mac towards the bed. "Lie down."

They fell sideways onto the mattress, breathless and laughing as the springs squeaked. Jez kissed Mac again. He couldn't get enough of it. Mac was so big and strong, sexy in a way that Jez hadn't fully appreciated before. As they kissed, Jez got his hands on Mac's fly and fumbled with the buttons, clumsily unfastening them so he could reach inside for Mac's cock. Once he'd got Mac's erection free, he did the same for his own, then started to stroke Mac in earnest.

"Oh," Mac gasped.

"Yeah." Jez's voice came out sounding wrecked. Mac's hot silky hardness in his hand felt amazing. He thrust his own cock against Mac's hip, hissing at the catch of rough denim on his sensitive cockhead.

Mac took the hint and wrapped his large hand around Jez, and Jez fucked into the grip of Mac's fist, biting back a moan.

It was messy and desperate, all biting kisses, stroking hands, and awkward thrusting. Jez was reminded of his first hand job—more enthusiasm than coordination, but it hadn't mattered because it was someone else's hand on his dick and that was all he'd cared about. Now this was hot because it wasn't just someone else. It was Mac, his mate, his *straight* mate, and this was all kinds of fucked-up and probably really unwise, but Mac was kissing Jez like he owned him, and apparently Jez was a total sucker for that.

He climaxed with an undignified whimper, slicking the tight channel of Mac's fist with warm come as he turned and pressed his face into Mac's neck. He didn't want Mac to see his expression. He was too raw, too exposed, afraid of what Mac might find there. As he shook with the force of it, Jez was dimly aware of the hot splash on his belly as Mac came too.

They lay panting for a few moments, the pounding beat of Jez's heart slowly settling as their breathing slowed. He drew back until he could see Mac's face. Mac's eyes were open, and his lips curved in a small smile. Jez wanted to kiss him again, but it felt like the moment had passed, and he was afraid Mac might not want that.

Instead, Jez closed his eyes and drifted, not ready to move yet. Still woozy from beer and come-drunk on top of the alcohol, he could have fallen asleep like that: sticky and half-naked on top of his duvet. But Mac moving brought him back to reality. Jez opened his eyes and watched as Mac sat up, holding his hand out in front of him and grimacing.

Jez chuckled. "I'm out of tissues, sorry."

The bed shifted as Mac stood. He pulled up his jeans and picked his T-shirt up from the floor and used it to wipe his hand. Jez lay unmoving. His cock was still out, wet and softening against his thigh, but he was too tired and fucked out to care as Mac stared at him in silence, his face hard to read in the dim light. A car horn sounded out on the street and broke the spell.

"I'd better go," Mac said.

Jez didn't want Mac to go yet, but he couldn't think of the right words to make him stay. He was too tired to be coherent. "'Kay… night."

"Good night." Mac closed the door softly behind him.

Jez barely had the energy to take his jeans the rest of the way off, find some clean boxers, and get under the duvet. Exhausted by drinking, dancing, and emotion, he fell asleep quickly — with a vague sense of unease about what they'd done and what it might mean for their friendship.

Chapter Nine

The rules changed again.

Now kissing was on the table, it stayed there, and watching porn together was a thing of the past. They still didn't talk about what they were doing, but there was an undeniable shift towards intimacy. Jez loved and feared it in equal measures, because as much as he craved Mac's kisses and the way he touched Jez's body with growing confidence when they got off, Jez couldn't shake the feeling that he was being swept along by something he couldn't control.

It still felt illicit. The secretiveness of this thing between them was an undeniable thrill to Jez. Yet at the same time, he craved more. Sitting next to Mac on the sofa, he longed for Mac's touch, for some casual affection, but Mac avoided touching him unless they were alone.

A few days after the night out, Jez headed for Mac's room to borrow a CD and caught Mac fresh from the shower with only a towel round him.

He knocked and entered after Mac's "Come in."

"Oh hey. Um…." The words stuck in Jez's throat as the sight of Mac—all wet hair, damp skin, and nipples tight from the cool air—wiped the memory of what he'd come in for. Jez licked his lips nervously, and Mac's eyes tracked the movement.

"Did you want something?" Mac quirked an eyebrow and the corner of his mouth lifted in obvious amusement.

The fucker. He clearly knew the effect he was having on Jez and was enjoying it.

Jez was still unclear about Mac's motivations. Mac was always enthusiastic about the physical side of their unspoken arrangement, and whenever they fooled around, he had no trouble getting hard or getting off. But there were definite limits that Mac didn't cross. He was good for kissing and hand jobs but had never used his mouth on Jez's cock, and neither of them had gone anywhere near each other's arsehole. Jez wasn't completely opposed to the idea, but he suspected it was way out of Mac's comfort zone.

"Jez?" Mac speaking his name snapped Jez out of his thoughts.

The heat in Mac's expression made Jez drop his gaze to Mac's crotch. Mac was half-hard, and the thick ridge of his dick was clearly visible through the towel.

Jez closed the door behind him and flipped the lock. They usually only did stuff when they were alone in the house or late at night when the others had already gone to bed. But it was early evening, and the house was busy with people. That knowledge only added to the thrill as Jez approached Mac, holding his gaze and raising his eyebrows in a question.

Mac answered him by grabbing his hips and pulling him close, his lips seeking Jez's in a kiss that stole Jez's breath as a dizzying lurch of arousal hit him like a punch in the gut.

Jez unfastened Mac's towel and let it drop, leaving him naked. Mac's cock reared up against Jez's belly, poking him insistently until he wrapped his fingers around its hot length. He smiled into the kiss and felt Mac smile back. Mac tugged at the hem of Jez's T-shirt, lifting it until they had to break apart so that he could get it over Jez's head. Mac smoothed his palms over Jez's chest, grazing the light sprinkle of blond fuzz. Jez wondered what Mac thought of it compared to his own smoothness. Did he like it? Or did it only serve to remind him that Jez wasn't a girl.

I'm not gay. Mac's words echoed in Jez's head. As far as he knew, Mac hadn't changed his opinion, but it didn't seem to stop him wanting to get his hands all over Jez.

"Get these off." Mac snapped the waistband of Jez's tracksuit bottoms, and Jez complied, pulling them down along with his boxers.

Facing each other fully naked for the first time in the glare of Mac's overhead light left them nowhere to hide. Two guys together, stone-cold sober, kissing and touching each other with no excuse apart from desire. However Mac justified this to himself, to Jez it felt pretty fucking gay, and he suddenly realised he was okay with that. More than okay, in fact.

He dropped to his knees and pressed his face into the juncture where Mac's thigh met his groin. He breathed in, smelling Mac beneath the soap. Mac's pubes were still damp from the shower and his balls had pulled up tight in the cool air. Jez licked them, and Mac drew in a sharp breath. Looking up, Jez licked up the underside of Mac's shaft. Mac stared down at him, his eyes wide and dark, mouth slack. Jez paused at the tip then circled it delicately with his tongue.

"Jez," Mac groaned. "Come on."

Staring up at him, Jez had the sudden realisation that although he was the one on his knees, he had all the power here. He'd always thought a guy in his position would be the submissive one, servicing the other, being used somehow. But now he was kneeling in front of Mac, it didn't feel like that at all. Mac wasn't taking anything from him, Jez was giving, and it was all on his terms.

"Stop teasing." Mac's voice had a desperate edge, and it sent a thrill through Jez, a flare of arousal so strong that his cock jerked and ached.

Jez stopped teasing… well, almost. A little teasing was fun, but he didn't make Mac wait too long to come. Another time it might be fun to draw this out for longer, but the floor was hurting Jez's knees, so he used all the tricks he knew to make it good until Mac's thighs were taut and trembling and his hips were moving, pushing his cock deeper as Jez encouraged him with enthusiastic sounds. Mac didn't warn Jez when he came, not verbally anyway, but Jez was ready for it because he knew Mac's signals now. He recognised the small, desperate sounds Mac made just before and the pulse in Mac's dick as he was about to shoot, and he carried on sucking Mac right through it.

"Jesus," Mac said as Jez pulled off. "That was fucking awesome. I thought I was going to black out there for a minute." He stumbled to the bed on wobbly legs and then sprawled out on his back.

Jez grinned as he stood. "That would be fun to explain in A & E."

Mac's gaze slid down to Jez's cock. "You really like sucking me off, don't you?"

Jez's face heated, but there was no point trying to deny it. The hard evidence curved up in front of him, proud and unashamed. "Yeah."

"Get over here." Mac patted the bed.

Instead of going to lie beside Mac as Mac probably intended, Jez crawled over him instead. Lust made him bold, and Jez straddled Mac's hips, his bare arse resting on Mac's softening dick as he started stroking himself.

"You turn me on," Jez said, the admission spilling out unchecked. "It's hot… having you in my mouth, making you come… I never knew it was something I could like that much." He was breathless, the sweet grip and slide of his hand pushing him close already.

Mac stared at him, his gaze flickering between Jez's cock and his face. Mac's cheeks had flushed and his eyes were half-lidded and sexy as hell. His expression didn't give much away, but Jez figured if he wasn't into this, it was up to him to say, or to push Jez away.

Mac didn't push him away. Instead he brought his hands up to Jez's arse, palming the globes of his buttocks, stroking and squeezing. He hadn't touched Jez like that before, and it felt dangerous, but so damn good at the same time.

Jez's cock throbbed, wet and slick in his hand as he jerked himself faster. The sound it made in the otherwise silent room was obscene. He moved his hips, fucking forward into his fist with a groan, and as he moved back, his perineum dragged over something hot and firm.

Oh God. Mac was getting hard again. Having Jez jerk off over him wasn't a problem, then.

Mac's obvious arousal sent Jez spiralling higher. He carried on, moving faster, fucking harder into his hand.

"Yeah, come on," Mac said hoarsely, and he readjusted his grip on Jez's arse. His fingers slipped into the crack where Jez was slippery with sweat, and a fingertip grazed over Jez's hole, first accidentally. Jez gasped, and Mac did it again, circling with careful, deliberate pressure as though he was testing to see whether Jez's body would let him inside. An unbearably sweet jolt of sensation surged through Jez, and he cried out as he came in a series of muscle-tensing, body-shaking pulses that left him weak and trembling. Legs aching and exhausted, he flopped forward onto Mac's chest, smearing his come between them as Mac slid his hands up Jez's back and held him tight as Jez slowly came back to earth.

"I'm gonna need another shower now." Mac's voice was warm, a low rumble in his chest.

Jez let out a huff of exhausted amusement. "I'll move in a minute," he muttered.

"That good, huh?" Mac sounded amused.

"Yeah." Jez wasn't capable of more than monosyllables. He loved being in Mac's arms. Mac was so strong and powerful, yet gentle too. The steady thud of Mac's heart vibrated through his ribcage. The beat was slow compared to Jez's, but as Jez lay there, the frantic beat of his heart gradually calmed, pulled into sync by the rhythmic *lub-dup, lub-dup, lub-dup* of Mac's.

Later that night, Jez showered before bed. As he soaped himself up and washed away the sweat and come from earlier, he paid more attention to his arse than he usually did. Curious, he probed his hole with a slippery finger and met resistance. Pressing harder, he managed to breach the ring of muscle with a fingertip. It felt weird—stretched and uncomfortable—and triggered the urge to push. But when his muscles acted reflexively, they softened and his finger slipped in further.

He hissed in surprise, tensing again at the burn and surprised by the strength of his muscles as they clamped tight around the intrusion. It didn't feel good exactly, but it didn't feel bad either. Mostly it felt strange. He imagined how it would feel if it was Mac's cock instead. He found it hard to believe taking something that thick could be pleasant, prostate or no prostate. But he supposed it must do, otherwise why would people bother?

Done with experimenting for tonight, Jez withdrew his finger, wincing a little at the sensation of it slipping free.

When he was tucked up in bed later with his laptop, supposedly researching geomorphological hazards for their current assignment, he took a sharp detour via Google.

How to have anal sex, he typed.

Overwhelmed by choice, he started at the top of the results and worked his way down the list for a while, skimming through the various articles and advice pages. By the time sleepiness finally overcame him, Jez had learned a lot. He wasn't sure whether he was ready to put his newfound knowledge into practice yet, but he couldn't deny he was intrigued.

Chapter Ten

The following evening was Friday. The house was quiet—they were the only two in again—and Jez and Mac had their books spread out on Mac's bed as they worked on their latest assignment. Mac had deliberately chosen a different essay topic to Jez. He welcomed Jez's help with planning but was afraid that if he picked the same question, they'd end up with work that was too similar.

They took turns to go through their notes, offering suggestions. Mac had done a good job this time, and when Jez told him he thought it was fine and that nothing needed changing, Mac gave a small, pleased smile.

"Really?"

"Yeah, it sounds like you have it covered," Jez assured him.

After that they started writing in earnest, trying to stay focused and challenging each other with word-count goals until Mac started yawning.

"My words aren't making sense anymore," he said. "I think I'm done for tonight. I need sleep."

Jez yawned too, stretching until his back cracked. He rubbed his eyes and realised how tired he was of staring at a glowing screen. "Me too."

He closed his laptop and started tidying up his books. Mac did the same, stacking them neatly onto his well-ordered desk.

Jez picked up his pile of books, paper, and laptop and headed for the door. "Night, then." He was a little disappointed they'd wasted the whole evening studying, but the work had needed doing, and he'd enjoyed Mac's company.

After dumping his books in his room, he went to the bathroom. When he emerged a few minutes later, Mac was waiting outside.

"It's all yours," Jez said.

Mac paused, and Jez clenched his fists to stop himself from reaching for him.

"Come back to my room... if you want?" Mac offered.

Jez was knackered, but he couldn't say no to Mac, not when he looked at Jez with that expression of hopeful vulnerability. "Okay."

Mac smiled, and the sight of it did weird things to Jez's belly.

Jez was glad nobody else was around to see him letting himself into Mac's room in his boxers and T-shirt. He got straight into the bed, shivering as the cold sheets slipped over his bare legs and arms. It was chilly today, and the heating in the house was always on low to save on bills. He turned away from the door and lay on his side with the covers pulled up to his ears, hugging his body for warmth. By the time Mac returned, the bed was warm and Jez was sleepy.

Mac turned the overhead light off, leaving only the dim glow of the lamp by the bed. The mattress dipped and squeaked as he climbed in. He curled his body around Jez and slipped a cold hand under the front of Jez's T-shirt.

"Fuck!" Jez started at the chill, but Mac's hand warmed quickly. A slow, lazy arousal hummed in Jez's belly, stirred by the rhythmic movement of Mac's fingers where they traced small circles onto Jez's skin and the hardness of Mac's erection pressed against Jez's arse. Any minute now, Jez would turn in Mac's arms for a kiss and reach down to stroke him, get his dick out, get him off… but this felt too good, and he didn't want to move. There was no rush. His eyes drifted closed, and he let Mac hold him, Mac's breath warm on Jez's neck, their bodies slotting together like puzzle pieces.

Jez woke a little later with a start. Disorientated in the darkness, the glowing red numbers of an alarm clock that wasn't his own—he always used his phone—told him it was just after midnight. He rolled onto his back. Still half-asleep, his brain hadn't quite caught up with where he was until his arm brushed a warm body.

Suddenly the events of the evening slipped back into focus. Mac had invited Jez back to his room… but then nothing had happened. Jez must have fallen asleep on Mac, and instead of waking him up and kicking him out, Mac had turned out the lamp and let him stay.

Jez sidled away, trying not to disturb Mac as he pushed the covers down on his side, about to climb out and creep back to his own room. But Mac threw his arm across Jez's waist and snuggled closer.

"Don' go." His voice was slurred with sleep. Mac put his head on Jez's shoulder, and the sweet, warm scent of his hair filled Jez's nostrils. Mac's arm was heavy, and Jez was too tired and too comfortable to put up much resistance.

"You sure?" Jez didn't want things to be awkward in the morning. Sexless cuddling wasn't normally their modus operandi, but Jez was into it. He was into everything with Mac, it seemed.

"Yeah. 'S nice." Mac's voice was a deep, contented rumble, like a giant cat purring.

It *was* nice, so Jez stayed.

In the morning it wasn't awkward at all. Mac woke Jez with a hand on his cock, and after he'd got Jez off, Jez returned the favour with his mouth — less mess to clean up that way, he figured. Plus he was getting kind of addicted to the feeling of Mac in his mouth, the fullness and the stretch, the sounds that Mac tried to stifle as he came.

Afterwards Mac pulled Jez back up the bed and pushed him onto his back, kissing him, lazily at first but then with building intensity. Soon they were both hard again. They stripped their clothes off between kisses until they were naked and grinding together. Jez let Mac do what he wanted, spreading his thighs and arching up against him, digging his fingers into the meat of Mac's arse and encouraging him to thrust. Mac pinned Jez's wrists to the bed and kissed him hard, his tongue pushing deep into Jez's mouth as their cocks rubbed against each other's bodies in a rough slide of almost-too-much friction on Jez's sensitive dick. It felt like fucking, the way they moved together, the growing heat and desperation.

Jez moaned, the sound almost lost in the kiss. He bucked against Mac, so close now and burning with it, cock aching and trapped against Mac's hip.

Mac grunted and came, making everything slicker and squelchier and infinitely dirtier. Jez tore his hand free from Mac's grip and worked his hand between them. He stroked himself furiously, hand wet with Mac's come, until his body arched and his orgasm ripped through him, leaving him gasping and shaking.

So much for less mess, he thought as he got his breath back. He chuckled.

"What's so funny?" Mac asked, lifting his head from where it was resting on Jez's shoulder.

"Nothing." Jez smiled, and Mac smiled back. He had a pillow crease on his face, but his short hair didn't look much different after being slept on. Jez's dark blond mop was probably like a bird's nest.

Mac kissed him again—a brief, sweet brush of lips and stubble that made Jez's heart twist in a way that freaked him out.

"You're squashing me," Jez said, squirming, then winced at the sticky reminder of what they'd just done as Mac rolled off him and cool air hit the mess on his belly. "You weigh a ton."

Mac snorted. "You weren't complaining a few minutes ago." His voice was teasing and intimate, and he still had a possessive hand on Jez's hip.

"Oh bollocks, look at the time." Jez glanced at the clock and then leapt out of bed. "I need to be at work in half an hour. I've got to hurry." He grabbed a towel off the back of Mac's chair. All was quiet in the house, and the bathroom was right opposite Mac's door. He didn't have time to waste with putting his clothes back on. "See you later, yeah?"

"Sure. Have a good day."

Jez spared one last glance at Mac. Naked and covered in jizz was a good look on him. The memory of it would see Jez through a long busy day in the café. He walked out of Mac's bedroom door, pulling it shut behind him, and nearly crashed into Josh. Josh had obviously just come upstairs, still wearing the clothes he'd left in the night before.

Josh's eyebrows disappeared under his dark fringe as he took in Jez's appearance. Jez's stomach was embarrassingly sticky, and he probably stank of come. He was blushing so hard, he felt as though he might combust.

"Good night?" Jez asked weakly.

"Not bad."

"I was heading to the shower…."

Josh's lips quirked as his eyes raked down Jez's body. "Probably for the best."

"Josh…." Jez said pleadingly. But he had no idea what to add. "This isn't what it looks like" wouldn't cut it, because it was *exactly* what it looked like.

"Chill, Jez. Your secret's safe with me. Mac's too."

The way he said it, Jez believed him. Weak with gratitude, he thanked Josh and scurried into the bathroom to scrub the evidence away.

When he went into his room after showering, Mac was waiting for him there, fully dressed and standing awkwardly by the bed.

"Who the fuck was that on the landing?" His tone was sharp, and his face pale and anxious.

A flash of hurt shot through Jez. *So this is how it feels to be a guilty secret.* "It was only Josh. Don't worry, he was cool. He won't say anything." Jez towelled his hair dry.

"Are you sure?"

"As sure as I can be." Jez went to his drawer to get out clean boxers. It felt weird walking around naked in front of Mac now that the playful intimacy of earlier had vanished.

"Good." But Mac still sounded doubtful. "We need to be more careful."

"Yeah, I guess." Jez yanked on his underwear, facing away from Mac. He didn't trust his face not to betray him.

It was chilly and drizzling outside, and as Jez hurried through the damp Plymouth streets, his heart was heavy. The shops were full of Christmas displays, all glitter and fairy lights and stupid, expensive gifts. The holidays were fast approaching. Only a couple of weeks left in the term before they'd all be going home for Christmas.

Jez sighed. Maybe a break from this weird thing he had going with Mac would be good for him. He felt stupid and angry with himself for the kernel of hurt in his chest that lingered after their last conversation. Of course Mac didn't want anyone to know about them. Hell, Jez wasn't ready to broadcast it either. But Mac's reaction to Josh catching them only served to reinforce the cold certainty that this thing between them was going nowhere. If Jez was truly honest with himself, what they had wasn't enough for him anymore. The sex was great, but it wasn't all about the sex for Jez now. Sleeping in Mac's arms last night had touched a part of Jez that no amount of hand jobs would satisfy.

After a stressful start to the day, things only got worse. The café was busy, Jez's boss, Helen, was in a foul mood, and everything that could possibly go wrong, did. Distracted, he kept messing up people's orders, and after the third complaint that involved a drink or a plate of food being sent back, Helen bawled him out in front of half the customers. Jez hung his head and didn't argue back. He knew he was in the wrong.

At the end of his shift, Helen called him into the office for a chat.

"I'm sorry I lost my temper earlier, Jez." She sounded as though she meant it. She wasn't usually one to lose her cool. "I'm having a bad day—well, a bad week, actually—but I shouldn't have taken it out on you. Anyway. There's no easy way to tell you this, but I'm going to have to let you go."

Jez stared at her in shock as the words sank in. "But—"

"It's not because of today." She was quick to reassure him. "And it's not just you. We're having to lay off both our part-time workers. But the café's in financial trouble, and the only way we can stay afloat is to make some staff cuts. We simply can't afford to keep you on. I'm sorry."

It was a small family-run place. Helen and her husband Paul both worked there, along with one other full-time employee.

"But it was so busy today. How will you manage?"

"We'll have to find a way. Me and Paul are going to work longer hours to make up for it."

"Okay. I hope you can make it work."

There wasn't anything else for Jez to say. But he was gutted. He'd liked working there. Helen was nice—on a good day—and Paul was an all-right bloke too. Jez would probably be able to find another part-time job eventually, but it might take a while. Plymouth was full of students looking for work that fitted around their classes, so the competition for suitable jobs was fierce. Not to mention the fact that half the graduates in the city couldn't get decent jobs these days, so they were working in bars and supermarkets too.

"Thanks, Jez. And if things improve and we have more hours for you in the future, I'll get in touch."

Chapter Eleven

It was raining again as Jez walked home, heavy drops that chilled his skin and dripped off his hair and down the back of his neck.

He stopped at Tesco Express on his way, bypassed all the Christmas shit, and headed straight for the alcohol section. He bought some beer he couldn't really afford — especially now — but he deserved something good after his shitfest of a day. As soon as he left the warmth and brightness of the supermarket, he opened one and started drinking.

As he walked, he wondered whether Mac had talked to Josh, or vice versa, and whether Mac was still freaking out about the morning. Jez was too low and distracted to care much, but he trusted Josh to keep quiet about it anyway. If Mac was in a state about it, that was his problem.

Jez got home to early-evening chaos at the house. Too many people in the kitchen, all trying to make things to eat before they went out and arguing over whose turn it was next to use the bathroom. Dani's boyfriend was visiting, so there was an extra person in the mix, which didn't help matters.

Jez put his unopened beers in the fridge and beat a hasty retreat to the living room where he found Mac and Josh watching TV. Josh was forking up noodles, and Mac was drinking something in a mug — so presumably non-alcoholic.

"Hi." Jez greeted them both and crossed the room to sit on the sofa next to Josh rather than joining Mac on the closer one.

"All right, mate." Josh nodded, a clump of noodles slipping from his fork as he glanced up at Jez.

"Hi." Mac gave Jez a quick, tight smile before turning his attention back to the TV.

Jez drank his beer in silence, watching Mac rather than the screen. A muscle ticked in Mac's jaw, and he picked at a loose seam on the arm of the sofa.

"How was your day?" Josh asked casually.

Grateful for the attempt at normality, Jez replied without thinking, "Okay." Then backtracked. "Well... actually it wasn't, really. I lost my job."

That got Mac's attention. He snapped his head around to look at Jez.

"Shit. Why?" Josh said.

"Yeah. They just can't afford to keep me on anymore."

Josh frowned. "I'm sorry. That sucks."

Mac still didn't say anything. He turned back to look at the screen again.

"Yeah." Jez took another gulp of beer. "So I need to look for something else after Christmas. There's not much work around, but I'll find something eventually. I'll have to."

Silence fell again. Josh's phone buzzed with a notification, and he read as he ate the last few mouthfuls of his noodles. As soon as he was finished, he stood.

"Okay, I've gotta run, or I'm going to be late."

"Hot date?" Jez raised his eyebrows.

"Something like that. Have a good evening, boys. Don't do anything I wouldn't do" — Josh glanced at

Mac, who had his gaze fixed on the telly again, and then gave Jez a wicked grin—"but that leaves you with plenty of scope."

Jez snorted, amused. "Fuck off."

Mac's ears had turned bright pink, and he was studiously ignoring them both. Jez hoped that Josh's teasing wasn't freaking him out too much. He was afraid it might scare Mac off.

Once Josh had gone, Mac turned away from the TV and faced Jez instead.

"Are you okay? About the job I mean?"

Jez shrugged. "I'll survive. I've paid off quite a bit of my overdraft already, and my parents will always help me if I ask. They won't let me starve." Not that Jez would ask them for help unless he absolutely had to. Having to admit the size of his overdraft to his parents back in the summer was one of the most humiliating experiences of his life. They'd sat down and made a plan for how he was going to repay it, and Jez was determined to stick to it, even if it meant living on the cheapest baked beans on toast for the rest of his student days. He also had student loans, of course, as everyone did these days, but he didn't have to worry about paying those off until he was in full-time employment. "Anyway, speaking of starving—I'm bloody hungry." Jez drained what was left in his beer. "I'm going to go and see what I've got in the way of food."

The kitchen was still mayhem. Shawn and Dani were fighting each other for space on the cooker top, and Dani's boyfriend was chopping things up for what looked like a stir-fry. Jez couldn't face the scrum, so he poured himself a bowl of Frosties and used up the last bit of his milk. He should have bought some food as well as beer in the shop; his shelf in the fridge was woefully bare.

"Is that your dinner?" Mac looked disapprovingly at Jez's bowl as he sat down again.

"It's fine. Cereal's fortified with vitamins, isn't it? I couldn't be arsed to cook anything. There's too many people in there."

Jez and Mac stayed in the living room as others came and went. Shawn joined them for a while to eat his dinner on the sofa, and then Dani and her boyfriend came to sit at the dining table with plates of whatever they'd been cooking.

Mac got up. "I'm gonna go and make some food."

The others left. On the way out, Shawn made a vain attempt to persuade Jez to join him and Mike at some new bar that had opened down by the harbour, but he didn't push when Jez declined, as usual. Once he'd gone, Jez was bored with what was on TV, so he went to join Mac in the kitchen.

"Do you want a beer?" Jez offered.

"Yeah, cheers."

Jez grabbed a couple of cans from the fridge, passed one to Mac, and then sat up on one of the worktops, watching Mac as he stirred something in a pan. It smelled delicious. Jez's mouth watered. The Frosties hadn't filled him up much; maybe he'd have some toast later.

"Whatcha making?" he asked.

"Tomato sauce for spaghetti. I stuck some bacon and mushrooms in there too."

"Nice." Jez made a mental note to go shopping tomorrow.

Jez drank his beer while Mac grated cheese, stirred his sauce and drained the pasta. But then Jez's phone buzzed with a text from his mum, so he wasn't paying attention when Mac dished up because he was busy replying—letting her know that yes, he was still alive, and yes, he was working hard and eating properly.

"It's ready," Mac said.

Jez looked up to see Mac with a steaming plate in each hand.

He stared at him. "Is one of those for me?" Mac had never cooked for him before.

"Who else would it be for?" Mac looked at him as if he was stupid. "If you want it. It'll keep it for tomorrow, if not... I just thought...."

"Yes! I definitely want it," Jez replied quickly. "Thanks." He slid down from the worktop and took the plate that Mac held out to him. Jez smiled, grateful, and the warmth in Mac's answering smile made a warm bubble of happiness expand in Jez's chest.

They sat at the dining table to eat and didn't bother to put the TV back on. They chatted about random stuff: their course, a test they had to study for, mutual friends. Every time their gazes met across the table, Jez felt another little twist of good feeling. He had to keep tamping down the urge to grin like an idiot.

After they'd eaten, they decamped to the sofa and put on a DVD of *Game of Thrones*. Jez used to watch it for the boobs as much as the story, but these days he found himself looking at the guys as much as the girls. Had his tastes changed, or was he simply more aware of his capacity for same-sex attraction now? None of them were a patch on Mac, though, he decided. He glanced sideways at Mac's profile, admiring his full lips and the square cut of his jaw.

Feeling bold, Jez sidled closer and put his hand on Mac's thigh. The hard muscle tensed for a moment and then relaxed. Without looking at him or saying anything, Mac brought his arm up and put it around Jez's shoulders. With a happy sigh, Jez settled in beside him and went back to watching the show. But with the warmth of Mac beside him and the weight of Mac's arm holding him close, he wasn't really following the story. His mind kept turning over with unanswered questions. How did he really feel about Mac? Was this a crush, or something more? And did Mac feel the same? Surely if this was just about sex for Mac, they wouldn't be sleeping together and cuddling on the sofa. But Jez wasn't brave enough to ask in case he didn't like the answer.

A sex scene on the TV finally captured his attention. It wasn't quite porn, but there was enough bare flesh and heavy breathing to get Jez turned on. It reminded him of how he and Mac had got together in the first place, and he wondered if it was affecting Mac too. He moved his hand on Mac's thigh, stroking slowly, gradually inching higher as the couple on the screen writhed, their bodies entwined. The man was thrusting into the woman, and she had thrown her head back in ecstasy. Jez's arse clenched as he imagined being fucked by Mac. Jez had indulged in a little solo experimentation in the shower again yesterday and found he could take two fingers quite easily. The thought of Mac's thick cock inside him made him nervous, but insanely horny at the same time.

Jez's hand reached the bulge in Mac's sweats. The rigid length of Mac's dick lay diagonally, trapped by his underwear. Jez thumbed the head.

Mac's breath caught, and Jez's cock jerked in response.

"Not in here," Mac said.

Jez met his gaze. Mac's eyes were nearly all pupil and his lips were parted. Jez couldn't resist leaning forward to lick at them, pushing his tongue between them in a messy, needy kiss.

Mac groaned and kissed him back, tightening one hand on the back of Jez's neck and bringing his other up to clutch Jez's shoulder and pull him closer. But then he pulled away again.

"Upstairs," Mac said, breathless now.

"Yeah."

For all Mac's protests, he couldn't keep his hands off Jez as he fumbled to turn the DVD off, and he let Jez take his hand to lead him up the stairs. They stopped on the landing again to kiss, all hot wet mouths and wandering hands as Mac guided Jez along. But when he went to open his bedroom door, Jez broke the kiss to say, "Can we use my room?"

A slight frown tugged at Mac's brows as he stared intently at him. "Does it matter?"

"I, uh...." Jez took a deep breath, his cheeks burning hot as he looked down at where his hands gripped Mac's T-shirt. "I've got some lube. I thought maybe we could try something new."

The silence felt painfully long, and Jez didn't dare check Mac's reaction. *Fuck.* He should have kept his stupid mouth shut. He'd probably overstepped some invisible line with the suggestion, and he'd messed up what had been a perfect evening until now.

"I suppose." Mac sounded uncertain. "But… which way round were you thinking?"

"Oh. I meant for you to fuck me... if you wanted to try that? Not that I wouldn't want to fuck you. Of course I would. I mean, why wouldn't I? But I didn't think you'd be into—"

Mac mercifully cut off Jez's nervous rambling with another kiss. Jez kissed him back enthusiastically, unsure of what the kiss meant but assuming it could only be a positive sign.

"Yeah," Mac finally muttered between kisses. "Hell yeah, I wanna fuck you."

Jez's knees went weak at the desperation in Mac's voice. Unable to wait anymore, he grabbed Mac's hand and pulled him towards his bedroom. "Come on, then."

Chapter Twelve

Jez turned on the lamp by his bed and got the lube and a condom out of his bedside drawer. He tossed them onto the bed where they lay, proof of what they were about to do. The mood changed. Desire was still there, but tempered with nerves. Everything felt new to Jez even though Mac's touch was familiar. They undressed each other slowly between kisses. Jez's hands shook with nerves, and Mac's didn't seem much steadier.

Finally naked, they got into the bed, and Jez gave Mac the bottle of lube.

Mac looked at it as though it was an unexploded bomb. "I don't know what to do. I don't wanna hurt you."

"You won't if we're careful. Well… it'll probably hurt a bit at first, but I want to try anyway." Jez heard the determination in his own voice. He couldn't believe he was asking for this. He'd come a long way in a few short weeks, but he wanted to do this with Mac, to have him that way. Then nobody could ever take that away from him—whatever happened in the future.

Mac still hesitated, so Jez took the lube from his hand and bent his knee. Lying on his side, facing Mac, he reached behind himself with slippery fingers. Jez circled his hole and then hissed as he pushed inside and felt that first burning stretch.

"Fuck, are you…? God. That's so hot," Mac said. His voice was husky.

"Wanna try? It's fucking awkward doing this to yourself anyway." Plus Mac's fingers were longer and thicker. Jez figured it would be good to take those before he tried dealing with Mac's dick.

Mac swallowed hard and nodded, seemingly lost for words.

Jez rolled onto his stomach and spread his legs for Mac, tilting his hips up. A momentary flush of shame flooded through him. It felt so dirty to be face down, arse up for another guy.

It's not just any guy, Jez reminded himself. *It's Mac.*

Mac pulled the covers down and knelt astride one of Jez's thighs. "Wow." His choked, appreciative voice swept all Jez's discomfort away on a tide of arousal. Mac gripped Jez's arsecheeks with warm hands and opened him further.

The first tentative touch of Mac's finger on Jez's slick hole made Jez's cock jerk and leak against the sheets.

Mac circled it slowly. "Like that?"

"Yeah." Jez's muscles twitched, and he arched his back, pushing against the pressure. "That's good. *Ahh!*" He tensed as Mac tried to push inside. Jez knew he should be able to do this, but it was different when someone else was in control. His body reacted instinctively, fighting it.

He forced himself to relax and was rewarded as Mac's finger slipped inside him. Jez tried to keep his breathing slow, remembering all the advice he'd read online. He turned to look over his shoulder. Mac was staring at Jez's hole, biting his lip and frowning in concentration as he moved his finger slowly in and out in shallow strokes. Jez flushed at the intimacy of it, the raw vulnerability of letting Mac touch him this way.

"That looks so…." Mac took a breath. "So fucking sexy. Jesus, Jez."

Jez let out a breathless chuckle. "I feel like a slut."

Mac met his gaze and his face softened. "You shouldn't. You're not." He moved his finger a little deeper. "I've been thinking about doing this with you, but I never thought you'd want to try it."

The awed expression on his face and the gentleness of his touch made something twist in Jez's chest. "Well, if you're going to have a gay experience, you might as well do it properly." He tried to keep his voice light, but it caught in his throat. "Put another finger in."

Jez wasn't sure he was ready for more, but he wanted Mac to stop treating him like glass. It was too sweet, too tender, and made Jez yearn for things he couldn't have. Jez wanted to get back to the heady desperation of wanting, taking, getting off. He knew where he stood with that.

But Mac seemed determined to go slow. He did give Jez another finger, but so slowly, so cautiously that Jez ended up pushing back onto them until they filled him—much deeper than he'd managed on his own in the shower. The pain was sudden, sharp and unexpected.

"Ouch," he hissed, freezing and panting, his fingers gripping the covers. Mac started to pull out. "No! Leave them there, but give me a minute."

"I thought we were supposed to be careful."

"I was." Jez huffed, half laughing. "You and your freakishly big fingers." Of course they weren't the only things about Mac that were big…. Jez's muscles clenched around Mac's fingers at the thought, but as he released, the pain subsided a little. The pressure remained, alien, and not exactly comfortable, but bearable. Jez hadn't expected anal to be this difficult. People did it in porn all the time. But no way was he going to back out now.

He moved experimentally, and it was still painful, but definitely not as bad.

"You okay?" Mac ran his free hand over Jez's hip and round to squeeze his cock where it had softened. "We can stop if you want. It doesn't feel like you're into this."

"No. I am... I mean... I want to keep going. Move your fingers. If you curl them down a little, then you should find my prostate. It's in there somewhere." Jez had managed to find it himself the other day, but it was awkward to reach with his own fingers.

Mac snorted. "Maybe you should have drawn me a map before we started."

"You've never found yours, then?"

"Not yet. Maybe I should try."

The image those words conjured up, along with Mac's hand stroking his cock, had Jez's flagging erection filling again. Then Mac's fingers rubbed him just right, finally finding that elusive spot, and sparks of sensation lit Jez up from the inside. "Yeah, there," he said. "God, that's good."

Mac kept going, gliding over Jez's sweet spot and jerking him off until Jez felt like maybe this *was* going to work after all. He wondered whether Mac was into this. Was he still hard? He turned to look at Mac again, and Mac's expression was intent and hungry. His cock reared up, thick and definitely ready for action. Jez shivered.

"You can fuck me now."

"You sure?"

"Yeah. Do it. Do me."

Mac snorted. "You're so classy." He withdrew his fingers, and Jez winced, it felt so strange as they slipped free. His arse clenched around nothing, feeling stretched and empty. Well, stretched was good, he supposed. He rested his head on his forearms and listened to the sound of Mac tearing open the condom.

"Bollocks, fucking slippery fingers…. That's it."

Then the warm weight of Mac's body covered Jez as Mac leaned over him and kissed his neck and shoulders, his hands stroking up Jez's flanks. Mac's hard cock poked Jez's balls, and Jez spread his legs wider.

"Come *on*." Jez was impatient now. His nerves were returning without Mac's hand on his dick, keeping him in the moment.

Mac guided him up onto all fours. His hands were firm on Jez's hips, and Jez let Mac move him how he wanted. He dropped his head and took a deep breath as he felt the firm nudge of Mac's cock at his entrance, gritting his teeth as Mac pushed in. Mac was so slow and careful again, but the grip of his hands and the shakiness of his breathing showed Jez how much the control cost him. Jez tried not to flinch at the discomfort, but he couldn't help himself.

"Do you want me to stop? We don't have to do this." Mac's voice was strained.

"No. Keep going." He could barely get the words out. Mac pushed in a little more and Jez flinched again, his muscles clenching involuntarily and making Mac gasp.

"I'm sorry."

"It's not your fault you've got a monster cock." Jez chuckled as he spoke, and the huff of breath he let out made something release. He breathed again, biting his lip as the pain subsided. "You were a terrible choice for my gay experimentation."

Mac didn't laugh, but he stroked his hands up Jez's back and back down to his hips, his touch gentle and soothing. "More?"

"Yeah."

Mac gave Jez the last inch, his hips finally flush with the back of Jez's thighs. "There," he said. "You did it."

Jez grunted, overwhelmed by the fullness, the thick stretch of Mac inside his body. It was so strange to be on the receiving end. He'd never stopped to think about how it felt for girls to be fucked.

Mac moved his hands again, stroking the globes of Jez's arse with a featherlight touch that sent shivers of pleasure up Jez's spine. "You okay?" he asked. "Can I move?"

"Only one way to find out." Jez knew he didn't need to ask Mac to be gentle. He'd been so careful, and that wasn't going to change now.

Mac started to thrust carefully, just tiny little movements of his hips.

"God," Mac said breathlessly. "That feels *incredible*. Now I know why so many guys are into anal."

It felt okay to Jez, but the earth wasn't exactly moving. The pain had almost gone, but he'd been expecting more sensation. "You can move more," he said. "It doesn't hurt."

Mac withdrew further on the next stroke and suddenly Jez realised what the fuss was about as the head of Mac's dick grazed his prostate, and then rubbed it again on the way back in. Heat rushed through his pelvis, radiating out from that spot in a flood of sensation. He gasped, and Mac paused.

"Too much?"

"No, don't stop. It's good…. Keep doing that."

Mac carried on, getting into a smooth rhythm that stoked that tingling warmth inside Jez. His cock was properly hard again now, hanging thick between his thighs, leaking precome, so he took his weight on one hand and moved the other to stroke himself.

"Oh fuck." The dual stimulation was intense, almost overwhelming.

Mac was breathing hard, letting out little grunts with each thrust. "Can you come like this?" he asked.

"I don't know…. Maybe?" It felt so different to what Jez was used to. The pleasure-pain of the stretch was good, but it was new and confusing to Jez's senses.

Mac's rhythm faltered. "I can't hold out much longer. It's too fucking good."

Jez jerked himself faster, chasing the elusive orgasm that lurked in his balls, at the base of his spine, growing and spreading but not quite taking hold.

"*Fuck.*" Mac thrust in deep one more time, taking Jez's breath away. Jez felt the pulse of Mac's cock as he came with a hoarse cry, his body jerking and his fingers biting into Jez's hips as he clutched him tight. "Fuck… I'm sorry," he muttered. "I couldn't stop."

"I'll take it as a compliment." But Jez was still breathless, wound tight, and painfully close to coming. He carried on stroking himself, but he couldn't quite get there. "Ugh." He groaned in frustration.

"Let me." Mac withdrew, slipping free from Jez's body with a wet sound that would have been embarrassing if Jez wasn't so focused on the need for release. He was dimly aware of the snap of the condom coming off, and then Mac's hands were on him again, guiding him to lie down and roll onto his back. Mac knelt between Jez's thighs and stared at his cock for a moment. Jez was hoping for a hand, or maybe Mac's fingers in his arse again—his muscles squeezed tight at the thought.

The last thing he was expecting was for Mac to lean over him and press a hesitant kiss to his balls, then another to the base of his cock. Jez held his breath, his body tight with tension and desperation. Mac drew back with an intense expression as he took Jez's cock in his hand and stroked it a few times before lowering his head and taking the tip into his mouth. Jez let his breath out in a needy moan at the wet heat and gentle pressure. He clenched his fists, toes curling as Mac licked and sucked experimentally as though Jez was a new flavour of lollipop he was trying out.

Mac's mouth on him, Mac's large hand stroking the base of his cock, his powerful shoulders between Jez's thighs—it was almost too much. Jez had been close for ages now, and as Mac rolled Jez's foreskin back and slid his mouth over the head, lips tight around the crown, Jez gasped. "I'm gonna come."

Mac made no move to release him, he simply flicked his gaze up, dark lashes and deep brown eyes pinning Jez, and that was it. Jez cried out, his whole body flooding with glorious release as he came. Mac took it, swallowing around Jez and carrying on sucking until Jez brought his hands up to Mac's face and gently pulled him away. His cock flopped wetly onto his belly, and Mac stared up at him, pupils huge in the dim light and his lips wet and parted.

"Come here," Jez whispered.

Mac crawled up his body and into his arms, and they kissed, passionately at first and then gradually becoming gentler, sweeter, until Jez's heart stopped pounding and his head stopped spinning. He was exhausted but exhilarated too, filled with a heady combination of excitement and fear. Tonight had brought everything into focus. There was no way he could pretend that this was still just about sex. Maybe it had been about more than sex for a while, but he hadn't let himself see it. He couldn't ignore it anymore, though. His feelings for Mac had raced about a million miles past friendship, and there was no going back for Jez now.

"That was amazing," he said honestly.

"Yeah." Mac followed the word with a final soft kiss to Jez's lips.

Jez wasn't brave enough to say any more. He sighed. How could he tell Mac he'd fallen for him? Mac was straight. Jez couldn't give him what he really wanted. This was buddy fucking, friends with benefits, straight guys experimenting—or not so straight in Jez's case, but Mac didn't know that. Maybe if Jez told Mac how he felt, Mac would feel that Jez had used him or tricked him somehow.

Mac yawned, and his arm over Jez's torso grew heavier as he relaxed. "Can I stay?" Mac murmured. "I'm too tired to move."

"Sure."

Mac rested his head on Jez's shoulder, and Jez brought his hand up to stroke Mac's close-cropped hair. It was like velvet against his palm, and Mac's warm breath ghosted over Jez's bare skin, slowing and becoming deeper as Mac drifted into sleep.

They'd crossed so many lines tonight. Jez's exhilaration was already giving way to unease as a little voice whispered that he ought to talk to Mac. In his heart, Jez knew he shouldn't get in any deeper, not when Mac didn't feel the same. But the warmth of Mac's body against his felt too good. With their arms wrapped around each other and their legs tangled together, it felt as though they were lovers. It felt real, and Jez could pretend he had what he wanted.

Just for tonight, he told himself. *I'll talk to him in the morning.*

Although he was exhausted, Jez lay awake for a long time. Anxiety niggled at the back of his mind, sending chilly tendrils through him, curling into his belly and tightening in a band around his chest. Beside him Mac snored softly, his body limp and as heavy as Jez's heart. What the fuck had he been thinking, getting involved with Mac like this? He hadn't been thinking—that was the trouble. The whole thing had been a slippery slope, and Jez had never been in control of it, not from the first time they'd wanked together.

Maybe he should put an end to it. If this was buddy fucking for Mac, then surely he wouldn't care much. His grades had improved with Jez's help, so there was no reason for him not to start going out and hooking up again. Jez's stomach lurched at the thought of Mac bringing someone else home, and the surge of nausea-inducing jealousy only served to reinforce his gut feeling that he should probably get out of this hole he was digging now, before he got any deeper.

Chapter Thirteen

Jez must have eventually fallen asleep and then slept soundly, because the next thing he was aware of was the sound of a sharp knock. He barely had time to register where he was and the position they were in — still snuggled up together in a sprawl of limbs — before he heard the door opening and Shawn's strident tones filled the peaceful silence.

"Hey, Jez. Sorry to wake you, but can I borrow your — "

They never found out what Shawn wanted to borrow. There was a pause, and then Shawn exclaimed, "What the fuck?"

Mac rolled off Jez so fast he took the covers with him. The cold air hit Jez's bare arse. He squawked and clutched at the duvet, yanking it back, but not before Shawn had probably got an eyeful if the muffled "Oh my *God*" was anything to go by. Jez rolled onto his back, shoulder to shoulder with Mac, and raised his head to see Shawn's shocked face.

"Jesus Christ, Shawn. Haven't you heard of knocking?" Mac growled.

"I did bloody knock." Shawn was still staring, his gaze flitting from one to the other of them. The expression on his face would be almost comical if it weren't for the situation. "But seriously. What the *fuck*?"

Jez didn't see much point in trying to deny it, but he still had no idea what to say. Mac was clearly having the same trouble.

Finally Jez broke the hideously uncomfortable silence with a lame attempt at humour. "If I told you we'd played strip poker and then fallen asleep, would you believe me?" He tried for a smile, but it probably came out more of a grimace.

Shawn carried on gaping. But Mac snorted, seemingly amused by Jez — fuck knew why.

"Yeah," Mac said. "And then it was cold, so we had to snuggle."

Jez burst into totally inappropriate laughter, and the nerves combined with the unexpected release of tension made him laugh louder and longer than the joke warranted.

Shawn shook his head. "You two are fucking crazy. I'm going to go and bleach my brain." There was an undertone of genuine disgust that cut through Jez's moment of hysteria and sobered him up abruptly.

"Fuck you," he snapped.

"No thanks." Shawn curled his lip. "That's not my scene. Didn't know it was yours either — or yours, Mac. You think you know someone…." He turned and left, slamming the door behind him before either of them could stop him, even if they'd wanted to.

"Bollocks." Mac was the first to speak. "Bollocks, arse, *fuck*!"

Jez didn't have anything to add. He resisted the urge to quip that that had been what had got them into this mess in the first place.

"I can't believe we didn't lock the fucking door last night." Mac was ranting now. "And who goes barging in on someone at" — he looked over at the alarm clock — "quarter to nine on a Saturday morning anyway? Fuck. I don't believe this is happening." Mac's face was flushed and he looked furious and upset.

Jez's stomach lurched. The reminder that he was Mac's dirty little secret didn't make him feel good at all. Not that he'd wanted to be open about it or anything, but he'd always assumed Mac had more invested in keeping it under wraps. It looked like he was right, from Mac's reaction to being outed.

"Let me go and talk to him." Jez pushed the covers aside and scrambled out of bed. When he moved, a slight twinge in his arse reminded him of what they'd done last night. "I'll try and catch him before he says anything to anyone." He grabbed his clothes and started to pull them on, desperate to cover his nakedness in the cold light of day. "I'll tell him it was nothing. That it was a one-time thing, that we were drunk and passed out after watching porn and jerking each other off or something. I mean, he'll still think it's *gay*, but that won't sound as bad, right?"

Jez was dressed now, and he met Mac's gaze. Mac's expression was tense.

"Um... yeah. Okay." His voice sounded strained. "Yeah. Tell him whatever you want. Whatever you think will help."

Jez went to Shawn's room, but he wasn't there. He cursed under his breath and then ran down the stairs, following the sound of cupboard doors slamming and the clatter of the cutlery drawer. In the kitchen he found Shawn and Mike. They were both dressed in sports clothes; Jez hadn't noticed what Shawn was wearing before.

Shawn had his back to the door when Jez entered. Jez was almost afraid to look at Mike. Had Shawn already told him what he'd seen?

But Mike looked up from the cereal he was pouring out, smiled, and gave him a cheery, "Hi."

There was nothing in his expression to suggest that he knew.

"Uh, hi. You guys are up early. What's going on?"

"We lost a bet last night, promised Katie off my course and her friend that we'd play squash with them this morning."

"Oh." Jez tried to summon up the will to smile. "I bet that'll be fun with a hangover."

"Well, at this rate we won't get to play, because Shawn's racket's broken. That's why he came to borrow yours. Shame you've lost it."

Relief flooded Jez as his suspicions were confirmed. Shawn had kept his mouth shut. "Yeah. You can probably hire one, though."

"Yeah." Mike picked up his bowl and headed for the kitchen door.

Jez waited till he'd gone and then pushed the door shut, wanting to make sure they weren't overheard. Shawn still had his back to him. He was standing over the toaster, glaring at it as though willing it to pop.

"Shawn, mate," Jez began.

"Don't," Shawn snapped. "I feel like I don't know you at all anymore. But whatever. It's not my business."

"Oh for fuck's sake." Jez's irritation flared. "I'm exactly the same person I've always been. What difference would it make if I was gay?"

"Are you?" Shawn turned then, and his face was hard.

Jez took a breath and paused a moment. "I don't know. I don't think so? But maybe I'm not totally straight either."

Shawn snorted. "D'ya think?"

"But anyway, the point is, me and Mac, it was just a one-time thing. We'd had a few beers and stuff happened. It was nothing. Nothing that matters." His gut lurched at the lie, because it did matter to Jez. But keeping their secret and protecting Mac mattered more. "So... please don't tell anyone, okay?"

Shawn stared at him. Jez felt each thump of his heart while he waited.

"Yeah," he said finally. "Okay. Like I said — it's none of my business anyway."

Jez guessed that was as good as he was going to get.

Once Shawn and Mike had left, Jez went back upstairs. His room was empty now, so he went to Mac's and tapped on the door. Mac grunted something that sounded like "Come in."

"Hey," Jez said.

Mac was fully dressed and lying sprawled in the middle of his bed. Jez sat awkwardly on the edge, and Mac didn't move over to make space. His face was shuttered and unhappy-looking.

"Stop stressing. Shawn's not gonna say anything." Jez was pretty sure they could trust him. He might be a bit of a twat sometimes, and he clearly had issues with what he'd seen this morning. But Shawn wasn't usually a troublemaker or a gossip. Jez didn't think he'd drop them in it with any of their other friends.

"Yeah? What did you say to him?"

"Like I said to you. I told him it was a drunken one-off. That it didn't mean anything and wasn't going to happen again. I thought that was best for damage limitation."

"Okay." Mac didn't look any happier.

"I'm sorry."

"What? Why?" Mac frowned, his dark eyes troubled.

"Well, it's all my fault, isn't it? That any of this happened in the first place. It was stupid. We should never have started it." Once Jez began talking, the words kept coming. He felt sick, but he knew it was for the best. It was time they put an end to this before anyone else found out and things got even more messy and embarrassing. "Let's call it a day, eh? It was fun for a while, but it's got out of hand." He forced out the last words over the lump in his throat. "I think it's best if we go back to being just friends."

Not that they'd ever officially been more than friends anyway.

"Oh. Okay, if that's what you want." Mac's face was impassive, but his voice caught. He cleared his throat. "It's probably for the best."

Jez nodded, his throat felt swollen and strange. "So, uh… I'm gonna go."

Mac lifted his hand as though he was going to stop him, but then he clenched his fist and dropped it back to the bed. "See you later, then."

"Yeah. See ya."

Jez's eyes prickled as he closed Mac's bedroom door behind him. *What the hell?* He'd never felt this sad about breaking up with a girlfriend, and he and Mac had never even given what they had a name.

Fuck. It really hurt.

On Sunday Jez hid out in his bedroom for most of the day, only venturing out to use the bathroom a couple of times. He was shocked at how miserable he felt. He tried to focus on studying, but he was distracted, going over the conversations they'd had that morning and questioning whether he'd done the right thing. But surely if Mac had wanted to carry on seeing — aka fucking — Jez, he would have put up more of a fight? And he hadn't protested. So, Jez must have made the right decision in ending it. It was better to get out now before Mac wormed his way any deeper under Jez's skin.

Finally in the afternoon, Jez was driven out of his room by hunger. He was in a state, still wearing yesterday's clothes with his hair sticking out in all directions, but he didn't care. He fixed some food — a tin of spaghetti hoops on toast — and took it through to the living room, where he found Mac, Shawn, and Mike playing *Call of Duty*. Mike was the only one who greeted him when he came in. Jez took his plate to the table in the window and focused on his food so that he didn't have to look at any of them.

The atmosphere in the room seemed normal. Mac was maybe a bit quieter than usual. Mike and Shawn were trash-talking each other constantly, but occasionally Mac would chip in. Jez wished he knew what the hell was going on in his head. He risked a glance at Mac and his heart twisted at the sight of him. As though he could read Jez's mind, Mac moved his eyes to meet Jez's. Their gazes locked for a moment, and something passed over Mac's face that matched the regret thickening Jez's throat, making it hard for him to swallow his mouthful of food.

Jez was the one to look away first. He forced himself to fork more food into his mouth, even though he could barely taste it.

Chapter Fourteen

The next week passed in a slow, lonely blur for Jez. He wasn't sure whether he was avoiding Mac or Mac was avoiding him—or a maybe bit of both—but the end result was the same. They hardly saw each other, despite sharing a house and being on the same course. It was amazing how easy it was to keep out of someone's way if you set your mind to it.

The city was swept by awful winter storms that lasted days. So, apart from scurrying to and from uni with his head down against the rain and gales, Jez spent most of his time holed up in his room wallowing in self-pity and listening to the windows rattle and the rain lash against them.

He lost himself in reading whenever he could. He started with book one of the Harry Potter series; they'd been his go-to comfort books since he was a kid. He figured that if it took him a couple of weeks to reread them all, he might be almost over Mac by the time he'd finished. Curled up in bed, with a battered copy of one of his old favourites in his hand, Jez could escape from his crappy reality for a few hours.

Jez missed Mac so much more than he would have expected. There was a massive, Mac-shaped hole in his heart, and Jez hadn't even realised Mac had filled that space until it—whatever *it* was—was over. Now they weren't hanging out anymore, he realised how much time they'd spent together. Studying on his own was lonely, and lectures were boring when he didn't have Mac to nudge and pass notes to. Even chilling out at home was crap without Mac for company.

He missed Mac physically as well as emotionally. He dreamed about him at night: about the strength of his body and the gentleness of his hands, about the sweet intensity of his kisses. Afterwards, Jez woke up hard in the small hours, with his cock aching as much as his heart. When he brought himself off, his head was full of Mac, and as he lay panting in the darkness after coming, he felt empty and unsatisfied.

The Friday after Jez had called things off with Mac, he was planning on trying to build some bridges. He was hoping the others would go out, so he could ask Mac to watch a film or play *Mario Kart* or something. He wanted to get back to a new sort of normal between them because the uncomfortable avoidance was making him miserable.

Jez hung around in the living room with Mac, Shawn, and Mike after dinner, waiting for the others to head out for the night. Dani was away again, and Josh was upstairs, presumably getting ready to go out as he usually did.

Shawn's phone buzzed, and he grinned when he read the text.

"Katie and Jess — our squash partners from last weekend — are going to be in the union bar tonight for happy hour, along with some of their friends. Sounds good to me. Are you in, Mike?"

"Sure."

"What about you, Mac… Jez?" Shawn asked. "Surely it's about time you reminded your dicks what they're for."

His voice was teasing, the tone light, but Jez's stomach lurched. True to his word, Shawn hadn't said anything to anyone as far as Jez knew. But the implication in his words felt like a veiled threat, an acknowledgment of the power he had over them.

Mike chuckled, but Mac kept his eyes glued to the TV. Only the tightening of his hand on the arm of the sofa betrayed him.

Jez tried to ignore the hot flush of anger that swept through him. Rising to the bait would only make Mike suspicious.

"Yeah, okay." Mac's voice was level. "I'm up-to-date with all my assignments for once. I reckon I deserve to get out."

Jez's heart sank. Of course Mac wouldn't want to stay in with him again, not after avoiding him like the plague all week.

"Gemma might be there," Mike said. "She's been asking after you ever since my birthday. What about you, Jez? You gonna join us for a change?"

Jez's gut clenched at the mention of Gemma, but he shook his head. "No. I'm still skint, remember, especially since I lost my job at the café."

"Not even for a couple?"

"No, sorry."

There was no way Jez could face an evening of watching Gemma hitting on Mac again. He gave up trying to finish the food on his plate, abandoned it, and left, passing Josh on the stairs and accidentally shouldering him as he hurried past to get to the privacy of his room.

"Hey. Are you all right?" Josh put his hand on Jez's arm, making him pause. Josh was dressed to go out in skintight indigo jeans, a leather jacket, and a T-shirt that would have been low enough at the front to show a lot of cleavage if he'd had one.

"Bad day."

Josh squeezed Jez's arm before releasing it. "I hope it gets better."

Not much chance of that, Jez thought, but he replied automatically, "Thanks. Have a good night."

Tucked away in his room again, Jez went back to reading. It was the only escape from his miserable thoughts. As he read he was occasionally distracted by the sounds of doors banging and footsteps on the stairs as the others got ready to go out. When all was quiet, Jez decamped to the sofa with a cup of hot chocolate and half a packet of biscuits. It was all he felt like eating. He pulled a blanket over his knees and lost himself gratefully in his book.

He wasn't sure how much time had passed when he heard the sound of the front door. His heart started pounding with anticipation: maybe it was Mac back early?

God, please let him not have brought a girl back.

He listened for the sound of voices, alert and tense. When Josh came in, alone, Jez relaxed. "Hey, what are you doing back already?" It was only half nine, according to the clock on the DVD player.

"I was tired." Josh sat on the sofa by Jez's feet.

He did look exhausted. There were dark shadows under his eyes that Jez hadn't noticed earlier on the dimly lit staircase. Jez's eyes tracked down, his attention drawn to a vivid mark on Josh's neck. He'd obviously got lucky before heading home. Jez flashed back to the memory of Mac and him kissing in the bathroom at the club just a couple of weeks ago. That had been such an amazing night. Jez had felt like they'd been poised on the brink of something wonderful. How had it all gone so badly wrong?

He sighed.

"Trouble in paradise?" Josh asked.

"Huh?"

"You and Mac." Josh's green eyes were too knowing. "You've both been miserable all week. It's obvious."

"Really? I mean… yeah. I've not been the best. But I thought Mac was okay. I haven't seen much of him, to be honest."

"He's not okay."

"Oh." Jez felt a small twinge of hope, which he quickly tamped down. Because even if Mac was missing him a little, it didn't mean they should start things up again. After a week, Jez still felt raw whenever he thought about Mac. What would be the point of rekindling their relationship—such as it was—unless it had some sort of future?

"You should talk to him." Josh made it sound so easy. "I think you're on the same page."

"It's not as simple as that. Neither of us is out. Mac's not even gay, for fuck's sake. He's very clear about that."

"Labels can be restrictive. Sometimes you need to stop thinking about gender and sexuality and focus on the person. If you care about them, if you feel good when you're with them, if you're hot for them… then what does any of the rest of it matter?"

"Try telling that to Mac."

"I could… but maybe *you* should." Josh yawned deeply, and then unfolded his slender frame from the sofa and stretched, showing a few inches of flat stomach and his hipbones where his jeans dipped low. "Anyway, I'm off to catch up on some sleep. Good night."

"Night."

Much later that night Jez was lying in bed, sleep eluding him as he went over the conversation with Josh. It made a lot of sense. But Jez couldn't help feeling it would be easier to be totally gay or totally straight. He couldn't imagine explaining his bisexuality to his parents, for example. But then he didn't need to—not unless he was ever in a serious relationship with another guy.

His drifting thoughts were interrupted by the front door opening and closing and the muffled sounds of voices downstairs. He could hear people moving around in the kitchen beneath his bedroom and someone else coming up the stairs.

The knock on his door startled him.

"Come in?"

Jez's room was in darkness, but the light from the landing showed Mac's broad silhouette as he paused in the doorway. Jez blinked, dazzled by the sudden brightness.

"Sorry. You asleep?" Mac's voice was a little soft around the edges from alcohol, but he didn't sound totally wasted.

"Obviously not. Are you coming in or what?"

Mac came in and shut the door behind him. He stumbled in the darkness, landing heavily on the edge of Jez's bed. He flopped down and rolled to face Jez, threw a heavy arm across him, and moved closer so that their foreheads were touching. His breath was warm and beery on Jez's face, and Jez wanted to kiss him so fucking badly.

Instead he asked, "What do you want, Mac?"

"You." Mac let out the word in a long sigh. He brought his hand up to curl around the nape of Jez's neck; the pad of his thumb pressed against Jez's racing pulse.

Jez tried to ignore the thrill of excitement and hope that surged through him. *It's not that simple*, he reminded himself.

It would be so easy to close the gap and kiss Mac, to get each other naked and give in to the raw, physical desire that Mac inspired in him. But that wasn't enough for Jez anymore.

Mac filled the silence of Jez's thoughts. "I only went out tonight because I knew if I stayed in, I wouldn't be able to keep my hands off you. I can't help it. I can't stop thinking about you — all the fucking time."

"Mac, please…." Jez didn't even know what he was asking for. This was all very good for Jez's ego, but terrible for his heart, because he wanted Mac to want him for more than his body, or his cock-sucking abilities, or his arse.

But Mac was on a roll now, and the words poured out of him, seemingly unfiltered. "I don't know what you've done to me, but you've broken my dick. We went to this club, and Gemma was all over me on the dance floor, and I didn't even get a little bit hard. All I could think about was your stupid face, and what it felt like that time I sucked you off, and how much it turned me on, even though I never thought I'd like it."

Jez tried again. "Mac—"

"And I missed you this week," Mac interrupted. "I missed you so much, and I'm crazy about you, and

I wish…. But I'm not gay, so I don't get it. Why do I feel like this?" Mac sounded so genuinely confused.

Jez had a lump the size of a fist in his throat. "What do you wish?" he whispered. His heart surged like a bird fluttering its wings against the cage of his ribs.

There was a long pause.

"I wish we could be boyfriends." Mac's voice was small and uncertain. "I know it's stupid and you don't want that, but—"

"Why do you think I don't want that?" Jez's voice came out more sharply than he'd intended. "I *do*. Fuck, I've wanted it for a while now."

"But you were so freaked out last weekend when Shawn caught us, and then you ended it…."

"Because I thought that was what *you* wanted. You were the one who kept insisting you weren't gay. I thought this was just a bit of fun for you."

"I'm *not* gay. Or I wasn't till the first time I kissed you. That was when everything changed." Mac's hand tightened on the back of Jez's neck. "Before that it *was* just a bit of fun. But after that night it was fucking confusing because it was so much more than that. It *is* more than that. So, can we try again?"

Jez drew back. He wished he could see Mac's expression in the dark. Mac sounded so hopeful, so sincere, and Jez's heart filled and overflowed as he smiled into the darkness.

"Yes." He closed the gap and found Mac's lips. He kissed him lightly. Their dry lips caught, and he tasted the faint sweetness of alcohol on Mac's breath. Mac's hand on the back of Jez's neck held him there, and he deepened the kiss for a moment before pulling back.

"So this is it. We're boyfriends now?" Mac still sounded uncertain.

Jez pressed his palm against Mac's chest and felt the answering thud of his heart. "Yep. Boyfriends who aren't gay." He chuckled.

Mac was quiet for a moment. "We're going to tell people now, yeah? And they'll all assume we're gay."

Jez shrugged. "Let them think what they like. Gay, bi, gay for each other, I don't care. Fuck labels. I'm into you and you're into me, and that's what matters."

Mac wrapped his arms more tightly around Jez and kissed his cheek. "Yeah. That's all I care about too."

Chapter Fifteen

On the last Friday of term, they threw an early Christmas party in their house before they all went their separate ways for the holidays. The party was on Friday night, and Jez and Mac were both heading home for Christmas on Sunday. Jez was dreading the impending separation but trying not to show it. They'd only be apart for a couple of weeks, and they could talk or Skype every day. He suspected Mac was feeling the same, though, because he'd been like a limpet in bed for the past few nights. Jez had got used to waking up with Mac plastered to his back every night this week. He'd miss it over the holidays.

The house was packed, the lights low, there were bits of tinsel draped around the place, and loud music filled the living room. Jez snuggled closer to Mac on the sofa and plucked the bottle of beer out of his hand. Jez had finished his bottle and couldn't be arsed to fight his way through the crowds to get another one. Mac turned and smiled, putting his hand on Jez's thigh in a possessive gesture that sent a little thrill through Jez. Being affectionate in front of other people was still a novelty. Jez didn't think he'd ever get tired of it.

Telling their friends about their relationship hadn't been as difficult as Jez was expecting. Word had spread fast, but it was better that way as it meant they had less people to tell themselves. Mostly, people had been pretty cool with it and seemed happy for them.

Shawn was still uncomfortable around them, but to his credit, he was trying now. When they'd told him they were an item, the first thing he said was "So it wasn't a one-off, then?"

Jez had fessed up to the lie, admitting it had been going on a while. Shawn snapped that he didn't need the gory details and proceeded to avoid them both for a few days. But gradually he'd chilled out and started behaving more normally again. There was still some residual tension on both sides, but Jez figured they'd get past it eventually. And if they didn't, then Shawn wasn't a friend worth keeping.

Jez had decided to tell his parents the day after he and Mac got it together properly. He was the sort of person who preferred to get difficult stuff over with, so the thought of waiting was worse than facing up to it. Mac wasn't ready to talk to his folks yet. He'd been apologetic, worried that Jez would see it as him not being as committed as Jez was. But Jez had reassured him that it was fine. It was Mac's decision to make in his own time.

Jez's parents had been better than he thought they'd be. But when they'd started to quiz him about it over Skype and he'd explained that he thought he was bi rather than gay, his dad had immediately started talking about it being a phase and something that Jez would grow out of. Jez shut that down fast and assured his dad that his bisexuality wasn't a phase, and even if he ended up with a woman, it wouldn't mean he was magically straight. He managed to refrain from adding that he was pretty sure no straight guy enjoyed sucking dick as much as he did.

His mum had been great, though. She was surprised, for sure, but quick to be supportive. She'd even asked if they could meet Mac sometime soon, so they had made plans for Mac to visit Jez's house for New Year.

Jez drained the last of the beer he'd pinched from Mac and then leaned in close, speaking directly into Mac's ear so that Mac could hear him over the music. "I'm gonna get another. Do you want one too?"

The light stubble on Mac's jaw brushed Jez's cheek as he replied. "Yeah, please. Guess I'd better, as some greedy bugger drank all mine."

Jez drew back until he could see Mac's face, and they grinned at each other. Mac licked his lips, and Jez couldn't resist leaning in for a kiss.

"Ugh. Get a *room*," Shawn yelled across at them, but Jez just gave him the finger and kissed Mac again, deeper this time.

Later, people were dancing. Dani dragged Jez to join them while Mac was in the toilet.

"Come and dance," she said. "You haven't moved from that sofa all night."

Jez let her lead him into the middle of the room. They'd moved all the furniture out for the party apart from the sofas, so there was a decent space. Packed tight with bodies in the dim light, it was almost like being at a club. Jez lost himself in the music for a while. He danced with Dani till her boyfriend came to claim her, and then he put on some stupid Dad-dancing moves with Mike for a while. While he was attempting to moonwalk, he felt firm hands on his hips as he backed into a solid body.

"What the hell do I see in you?" Mac's amused voice in his ear made Jez shiver.

Jez turned, putting his arms around Mac and reeling him in. "You're just jealous of my legendary dance skills. Stop laughing at me." He kissed the smirk off Mac's face.

They carried on dancing, together at first, but then they drifted apart in the throng for a while. Jez was dancing in a group with Josh, Dani, and her boyfriend when he caught sight of Mac with Gemma. She had her arms around Mac's neck and there was no space between their bodies. Jez frowned, jealousy flashing through him and making his muscles tense.

As if Mac could feel the heat of Jez's glare, he turned his head and met Jez's gaze. He grinned and jerked his head in a come-here gesture.

Gemma peeled herself off Mac when Jez sidled up. "I was only borrowing him," she said with a wistful smile. "You can have him back now."

"Thanks." Jez tried not to sound pissy, but he wasn't sure he'd managed it.

Mac reached out a hand and grabbed Jez's wrist, tugging him closer. He wrapped his arms around Jez, and they swayed to the music together.

"You don't need to be jealous," Mac murmured in Jez's ear.

"I'm not."

"Liar. If looks could kill, poor Gemma would be toast. We were only dancing. And anyway... you're the one I want, not her."

A flood of heady possessiveness washed over Jez, making his cock thicken and swell in his too-tight jeans. "Good, because you're *mine*."

With their hips aligned and only a couple of inches of height difference Jez could feel Mac's bulge nestled above his own. Neither of them was totally hard yet, but they were getting there.

"Wanna go upstairs?" Mac spoke the words quietly into Jez's ear.

Jez turned his head and claimed Mac's lips in a deep, dirty kiss. Mac kissed him back, his hands wandering down to grab Jez's arse. Jez was breathless when Mac finally pulled away to ask, "Was that a yes?"

"Technically, it was a hell yeah."

Mac laughed, already taking Jez's hand and dragging him towards the door.

Upstairs, they stumbled into Jez's room and locked the door behind them. They'd learned their lesson about privacy the hard way.

Jez pinned Mac against the door, kissing him impatiently now. They fumbled at each other's clothes, tugging up T-shirts, unbuttoning flies, and kicking off their shoes. Mac pushed back against Jez, backing him towards the bed as they discarded their T-shirts. Mac's skin was warm from dancing, with a light sheen of sweat that helped Jez's hands glide over the muscles of his back. Jez kissed down Mac's neck, breathing him in. They stumbled towards the bed and then tripped and fell in a tangle, laughing between kisses, landing with Mac sprawled on top.

Mac broke the kiss to peel Jez's remaining clothes off and then stood to get his own jeans and underwear off. His eyes lit hungrily on Jez's hard cock, which jerked in response as though asking for attention. Mac grinned, crawling back over Jez to press tantalising kisses to his thighs and hips, deliberately avoiding Jez's straining erection.

"Fucking tease." Jez put his hand on his cock and started to stroke. "I'll do it myself if you won't."

Heat flared in Mac's dark eyes, and he licked his lips. "Yeah?" His voice was husky, and he stared at the movement of Jez's hand, entranced.

"You like that?" Excitement curled at the base of Jez's spine as he gripped tighter, thumbing over the sensitive head with each stroke. "Want me to put on a show for you — for old time's sake? Or maybe we should watch some porn?" He grinned, breathless.

"Who needs porn when I can watch my real-life boyfriend getting himself off?" Mac asked, his gaze still fixed on the slow, steady movement of Jez's hand.

"You do it too."

Mac moved to straddle Jez's legs, his powerful thighs braced and his thick cock rearing up. Mac wrapped his hand around his shaft, and Jez watched as he jerked himself, slowly at first, then gradually increasing the pace as his breathing grew shallow and ragged.

"So fucking sexy," Jez said. "I always loved watching you. Right from the start, even when I shouldn't have been looking."

"Me too. I was afraid you'd notice I was looking at you instead of the porn." Mac paused for a moment. He dipped his fingers in his slit and spread the shiny slick over the head of his cock before starting to stroke himself again. Mac's balls were high and tight. Jez could feel his own orgasm coiling in the pit of his belly, the tension building fast. Caught in a feedback loop of arousal, the only sounds in the room were their breathing and the wet slide of hands on cocks.

Mac was the first to come. He groaned, thighs tensing and abs rippling as he shot his load all over Jez's cock and his moving hand. The warm wetness slid between Jez's fingers as he carried on stroking himself and the dirty-hot rightness of it sent him over the edge too, crying out as pleasure ripped through him, leaving him cursing and jerking helplessly, his cock pulsing and adding to the come that already covered him. Jez closed his eyes, lost for a moment, until his heart stopped trying to beat its way out of his chest. His hand was still curled around his cock as it began to soften and shrink.

A gentle finger traced through the sticky mess on Jez's belly. He squirmed, ticklish, and opened his eyes to see Mac gazing down at him. His eyes were soft now, full of emotion that made Jez's stomach flutter.

"Wow," Mac said, and his mouth curved in a small smile.

"Yeah."

"That was a million times hotter than any porn I've ever watched."

"Same." Jez was still too fucked out to manage more than monosyllables.

Mac laughed softly. "You're a mess." He reached for the tissues by the bed, passed one to Jez for his hand, and cleaned their combined mess off Jez's belly as best he could. Jez lay there and let him. He liked being looked after.

"Wanna go back down to the party?" Mac asked.

The deep bass of the music was still vibrating through the floor. It would probably go on for hours.

"Nope. I want you all to myself."

They got under the covers, still naked and a bit sticky, and curled up in each other's arms to trade lazy kisses.

Jez was drifting on a cloud of bliss. Their impending separation was a tiny niggle at the back of his mind, but it wouldn't be for long. And right now, with Mac wrapped around him, it was hard to feel anything other than happy.

Jez was almost dozing when Mac said quietly, "Jez… I think I'm in love with you."

Jez's heart surged, but he kept his tone light. "You think? How about you get back to me when you're sure."

"Fuck off," Mac huffed. "I've never felt like this before, so it's confusing, okay? But yeah, I'm pretty sure."

Jez smiled against Mac's shoulder where his head was resting. Normally a man of few words, it was adorable when Mac babbled. It only happened when he was nervous.

"I wanted to tell you before we go home for the holidays," Mac continued. "So you know how into this I am. You don't have to say it back…. I just wanted you to know, so—"

"Mac." Jez finally cut him off, lifting his head so he could see Mac's face. "I've been in love with you for weeks, you idiot. I'm glad we're finally on the same page."

Mac's smile was radiant. "Me too."

Jez put his head back on Mac's chest, and they were silent for a moment.

"So…," Jez began. "At New Year, if my mum wants to know how we got from being friends to boyfriends, what are we gonna tell her?"

Mac snorted. "Oh God, will she ask?"

"Probably. She's dead nosey."

"How about… we tell her I was struggling with a particularly *hard* assignment one night, and you gave me a helping hand, and then one thing led to another."

"Technically, I think the first time, I gave you a helping mouth." Jez chuckled, then snuggled closer and closed his eyes. "But other than that, it's the perfect cover story. Let's run with it."

About the Author

Jay lives just outside Bristol in the West of England, with her husband, two children, and two cats. Jay comes from a family of writers, but she always used to believe that the gene for fiction writing had passed her by. She spent years only ever writing emails, articles, or website content.
One day, she decided to try and write a short story — just to see if she could — and found it rather addictive. She hasn't stopped writing since.

www.jaynorthcote.com
Twitter: @jay_northcote
Email: jaynorthcote@gmail.com

If you enjoyed *Helping Hand* you can read Josh's story in *Like a Lover*, coming September 2015

Also by Jay Northcote

Cold Feet
Nothing Serious
Nothing Special
Nothing Ventured
Not Just Friends
Passing Through
The Dating Game
The Little Things
The Marrying Kind
Top Me Maybe?

Free short stories:
First Class Package
Passing Through

Audio Books:
Nothing Serious
Nothing Special
Nothing Ventured
Not Just Friends
The Dating Game
The Little Things

Made in the USA
Charleston, SC
30 November 2015